Also available on Amazon from Ember Pepper

Sherlock Holmes and the Crawling Chaos
Sherlock Holmes and the Ghastly Gate
The Adventure of the Threatened New Yorker
The Specter at Painswick
The Byrne House Murders
Mary

Coming Soon:

The Case of Castle Atkinson
Sherlock Holmes and the Court of Time

Mysteries in Gaslight:
The Secret Cases of Sherlock Holmes

In my long association with Holmes, we had encountered murderers, robbers, scoundrels, and frauds both in England and on an international scale. However, one personage who crossed our threshold left him more unsettled than I had ever seen him. Until now, I had kept this particular tale off the page, sensitive to Holmes's feelings and averse to causing him embarrassment. However, twenty years hence, I know Holmes looks back on the affair with a sort of resigned amusement that only time can foster.

It was May of 1901, and Holmes was at his writing desk distracting himself from his current monograph by falling deeply engrossed in the morning edition of *The Gloucester Journal*, one of dozens of papers he had delivered every day. He emerged only to begin a virulent, albeit justified, tirade against the police and their handling of the murder of another unfortunate woman in Whitechapel. "Have you seen this drivel, Watson? This poor girl was brutally murdered in the most horrific manner, and the police are bungling everything."

He twisted in his chair and tossed the journal on the morass of newsprint covering the middle of the sitting room floor. I leaned over the arm of my comfortable armchair and swiped the paper up to see what had so soured my friend's mood.

MURDER IN A WHITECHAPEL LODGING HOUSE

"Within a stone's throw of the house in which Mary Kelly was murdered and mutilated in November, 1888, when police and public alike were staggered by the extraordinary series of atrocities known as the Ripper murders, a tragedy of a somewhat similar character occurred in the early hours of Sunday morning."

I sighed, a feeling of resignation washing over me. "Do you think it's him?" I asked quietly.

Holmes didn't answer at first, staring resolutely down at the blank paper of his yet-to-be-started monograph on matching specific blood spatter patterns with types of violence, his gaze turned inwards.

Finally, he gave a small shake of his head. "No, it's not *him*. He's dead."

He said no more, applying himself to his task with a concentration that seemed specifically designed to discourage conversation.

"Will you look into the case?"

"My services have not been requested."

"That's never stopped you before."

"There's a more interesting story on page 2."

I glanced at it. A man had been found hanging from the iron fence of the London Royal Hospital.

"Why leave a body in such a public manner?" Holmes asked. "It may have some meaning that I think is curious."

"How is this any more unique than the murder of Mary Ann Austin?"

"Because it means there is a third party at play – whoever the message was for. Besides, as I said, the police have not tried to consult me about the woman's death."

Surprisingly, it seemed he did not wish to be consulted, but before I could wonder too much at this, we heard the step of our landlady ascending the stairs, followed by a quieter click of heels.

Mrs. Hudson peeked her head around the door. "Mr. Holmes, I know you asked not to be bothered, but there is a young lady here that seems desperate to see you if you could spare a moment."

Holmes sighed, tapping his pencil against his paper before throwing it down irritably. "I'm getting nowhere with this. Let the lady in, Mrs. Hudson. A distraction may be a fine thing right now."

He stood and bent down to gather the mess of papers into a pile to clear a path for our guest. I stood as a woman of about 30 years of age stepped into the room, nodding her thanks to Mrs. Hudson as she closed the door behind her. She was a pretty girl, with a very unique shade of dark brown hair and elfish features. She smiled politely at me, revealing a very pleasing dimple in her right cheek.

She gave me a small, awkward curtsy as if someone had told her it was a customary thing to do and waited to be given permission to sit. In my long acquaintance with Holmes, I had learned something about deduction and recognized immediately by the faded patches of her skirt near her knees and the faint remnants of coal dust along the edges of a few of her fingernails that she was likely a housemaid.

Holmes turned, his hand already raised to welcome our guest into our usual client's chair when he saw her and drew up short. His face paled with what I could now easily recognize as mortification, his stance suddenly tense.

I looked between the two, confused. It seemed my friend knew this woman, but she made no indication that she had ever met him before. She frowned a bit at his behavior, glancing at me.

Braving through the discomfort of the moment, she smiled. "Your landlady told me that you did not want visitors, so I'm sorry to interrupt, but it's very important that I speak to you. I need your help, Mr. Holmes."

Holmes still said nothing. My gaze shifted back and forth between them in a way that I'm sure would appear comical from an outside view. I imagined a gigantic puppet master twisting my little wooden head to and fro for a delighted audience.

The awkward tableau was becoming unbearable. I had finally decided that I would be polite and urge her to sit when Holmes seemed to shake himself free of whatever horror had gripped him. "You need my help?" he echoed. The response struck me as quite dumb, particularly for Holmes, and I gaped a bit at him in shock as he finally gathered his wits.

He cleared his throat. "Of course, forgive me. My mind was elsewhere. Please sit."

Once settled, Holmes stayed silent for a painfully long moment, and I decided to begin the interview if only to save us from this torture.

"I'm Doctor Watson," I said kindly. "This, as you evidently know, is Mr. Holmes. Can you describe your problem for us?"

She nodded, appearing relieved to have some concrete directions. "Yes, it's a pleasure to meet both of you. My name is Agatha Davis. I was born in Whitechapel but, because my mum had a problem with drink, I went to live with my uncle, my mum's brother-in-law, whose home was a bit more stable.

He died, though, when I was twelve, and I went back to my mum who, by that time, had eased off the drink and was doing better. Like many young girls, I quickly went into service as a maid. I served in one household for about 13 years before the couple passed, and then I went to work for a man. You may have heard of him - it was in the papers about two years ago - Mr. Milverton? He was shot in his home, but his murderer was never found." She glanced between us in question.

I nodded idiotically, my face flushing a bit even though I had nothing of which to be guilty. I snuck a glance at Holmes and saw he was blushing as well, trying valiantly to look as if he did not notice my stare.

"Yes," I confirmed, my voice a bit scratchy, "I think I read something of it." At my own words, I felt an inescapable burst of irrational laughter crawling up my throat that I just barely repressed.

Thank the heavens that the girl did not seem to notice. She continued on, "It was not a personal loss. He was a horrible man, but it did mean I no longer had a position there. After that, I went to work for a young man on Harley Street, you know where all the doctors live. I still work for him. His name is Dr. Chambers."

I gave her a curious frown. Not quite able to stop myself, I asked innocently, "Pardon the inquiry, but you never married?"

Holmes made a noise in his throat that I took as a warning, but I pretended I did not hear it.

She smiled prettily. "Oh, no. I had a few suitors, but none of them went as far as marriage. It's all right, in any case, I live with Dr. Chambers and visit my mother at the end of the week. I have more than most, I suppose. This brings me to my current problem." A sadness crossed over her face. "I said that I visit my mother, but I should have spoken in the past tense. You see, she was murdered yesterday." She swallowed back a well of tears. "I went home to her little room on Dorset Street, and found her on the floor. The police think she was strangled, but they don't want to help because people die all the time in Whitechapel."

"So you wish us to investigate?" I asked.

"Yes but, I beg your pardon, I'm not finished, doctor. After her death, as

I was walking along the street to Dr. Chambers' home, two men sprang from the darkness between the trees and tried to carry me off. I fought hard and bit one of them on his hand. When he let me go, I kicked wildly and managed to scream while running down the lane. Dr. Chambers heard and opened the door to let me in. He went out to find the men, but they were already gone. He told me not to leave the house again until we knew it was safe, but I had to come see you."

"That must have been very scary for you," I commented, feeling increasingly out of my depth as Holmes had still not said a word.

I turned my gaze to him pointedly.

He cleared his throat and stood up abruptly. "I cannot look into this personally."

Her face fell. The pathetic look of absolute dismay seemed to have some effect on the detective. His teeth clenched and then he gave an inch, "I will contact the police in charge and see what I can find out for you. That is the best I can do at this moment, Ag- Miss Davis."

She perked up at that. "Here, I have a note with my current address on it. Please tell me if you have any information." She pulled a torn piece of writing paper from the cuff of her sleeve and held it out. The action forced Holmes to lean over to take it, coming close to her. At the proximity, she frowned and gave him a probing look. "Have we met before?"

He shook his head firmly. "No. No, not at all. I understand this matter is of great importance to you. I'll do what I can." It was an obvious dismissal, so she stood and thanked us profusely if a bit confusedly, taking Holmes's hand without asking and pressing it between hers warmly. The detective endured the action with unease, and she swirled from the room.

An oppressive silence settled over us in her wake.

I let out a chuckle. "Well, she is delightful."

"Watson," he warned.

"Holmes, I do think she recognized your smell!"

His face grew even redder, and he turned his back, fiddling with the papers on his desk. "She did not," he countered. "That's impossible."

"Mmhhmmm. I presume you do not mean to confess to her, so I'll try my very best to keep myself under control-"

"I'm not taking her case."

"What? Holmes, she needs your help. You *owe* her that much."

"I owe her nothing," he snapped, but he stared down at the address she had given him for some time before folding it and putting it into his pocket.

"I don't agree with this, Holmes. It seems in poor character to refuse her."

"Your objections are noted."

This argument seemed a dead end. I was disappointed in my friend, but I strove to be understanding of how uncomfortable the situation was for him.

"I'm frankly shocked she did not recognize you," I said instead.

"My disguises are professional, Watson, as you know. Coupled with dim lighting, they are impenetrable."

"Yes, but …." I trailed off.

"But what?" he challenged.

I cleared my throat. "It's just that you courted her to the point of engagement."

"And?"

I fluttered my hands in affected disinterest. "Nothing, never mind."

He pressed his fingers to the bridge of his nose. "Good god, I thought she was here to confront me. I never imagined I'd see her again."

"You assumed she'd disappear into the great mire of poor people, never to be of concern to you again?"

A look of startled hurt painted his face. I'm not sure why I said it. I knew Holmes never looked down or disregarded anyone due to their status in society. He was simply not that sort of man. But his nonchalance about his own cold-hearted ploy with the woman had always chafed at me. It was unlike him, driven by his obsession with ridding the world of Milverton.

He glared at me and then, in a flurry of sudden energy, he twisted on his coat and swept up his walking stick. "Come, Watson. Don't let me brave Whitechapel alone."

I stood to follow. "So you will take her case?"

"Indeed not. I want to find out who was left hanging from that fence a few days ago."

Holmes's stubbornness here was inexplicable to me; he was adamant, in my opinion, to choose the mystery that seemed the least remarkable. I understood his reticence in the matter of the delightful Agatha, abandoned fiancée, but the revolting murder of Miss Austin seemed most vicious and worrisome.

I followed, keeping my opinions to myself for now.

The police in Whitechapel were notorious for various reasons. Not the least, the failure to catch the Ripper. Before that, they had garnered a reputation for being overworked and, therefore, a bit lax in their investigative policies. Holmes had had trouble with them before, irritated by the disdain with which they treated the very community they were meant to protect. Now we met with an Inspector Lockhart who, while not overtly contemptuous, seemed annoyed that we were bothering him.

"Forgive me," he said as we shook hands, "But we are understandably busy, as always. I can't imagine what could draw you here. Your skills are renown, so I can't see why you'd lower yourself to apply them to the mundane crimes of the East End."

"On the contrary, sir, I spend a great deal of time here," Holmes answered. "The lovely denizens of Whitechapel have so few to advocate for them. I do what I can."

If the inspector noticed the subtle censure, he didn't show it. He only said, "Well, what can I help you with?"

"Three days ago, you discovered a man hanging from the fence of the hospital on Whitechapel Road. This seems a strangely public display, and it piqued my interest. Are you holding the body?"

"I'm afraid you're too late for that, Mr. Holmes. We buried him yesterday."

"Who was he?"

"No way to identify him. No one came forward."

"It seems you could have given it more time."

"We needed the mortuary space."

Holmes visibly reigned himself in. "Are you in possession of any of his effects? Or did you burn them?"

Inspector Lockhart bristled. "I'm not pleased with your implication, sir. We do what we can here. Austin's murder is pressing - just because the Ripper has taken a break, does not mean he isn't still out there. In any case, the unidentified man's possessions, as well as the rope he was hanging from, should still be at the Shoreditch mortuary in one of the boxes, if the coroner has not disposed of them yet."

Holmes nodded and, without bidding him a good day, spun on his heel to leave.

The day was pleasant, so we walked the short distance to the mortuary which was a small rectangular building next to St. Leonard's Church. Holmes stood staring at the door for a moment before entering. We were met with Henry Wilton, a man just beyond the threshold of 80 who had been the undertaker during the inquest of Mary Kelly and who had, reportedly, paid for her burial. There were two bodies on rickety tables cramped together, both covered by sheets that had seen better days. Holmes studiously ignored them.

Holmes shook the man's hand. "Wilton," he nodded respectfully. I had never met the man, but it seemed obvious Holmes had had some dealings with him and viewed him with upmost respect.

Henry Wilton seemed equally deferential. "Detective," he said warmly, "I am pleased to see you, though I know you must be here on business. No one enters the mortuary for recreational purposes."

"Certainly not," Holmes murmured. "I hope you can help us. Inspector Lockhart says you handled the body of the unidentified man found at the London hospital?"

"Oh, yes. Strange affair. I protested how quickly they discarded the body. I know those who pass my doorway aren't Lords, but we could at least see if they have family. In any case, if you wanted to examine him, he's in the earth now, Mr. Holmes."

"Yes, so I was told. Do you he his effects?"

"You're lucky. I have not disposed of them yet." He moved to a crowded corner of the room and shifted through some boxes, some tin and some old repurposed bandboxes. "Here you are." He put a faded floral hat box on the small wash table and opened it.

"There is little here," he explained. "He had nothing on him but his clothes and this pocket knife. The rope is the one found around his neck."

Holmes examined the knife. "This is a sailor's knot knife."

"That's what I thought as well," Wilton agreed. "But the police did not seem too interested."

"This rope is very telling," Holmes said, peering closely at the knot on the noose. "It's a Portuguese bowline. Sailors use this to make a boatswain's chair. Clearly the victim and the murderers are sailors of some sort. I doubt the official navy; this knife is not a navy issue, but it is very well used."

He handed me the rope, a habit he had formed after years of allowing me to tag along. I doubted I could provide any helpful insights, but I dutifully turned it over in my hands.

"It is wire rope," I pointed out. "Often used on ships."

"That seals it," Holmes said, returning the items to the box.

"It doesn't seem very helpful, if you don't mind me saying," Wilton offered. "How do you find one sailor in a town with a port as busy as London's?"

"I've done it before," Holmes said simply. "Thank you."

Though he seemed eager to quit the morgue, he faltered, staring at the two sheet covered bodies.

"Is one of these women named Davis?" he asked reluctantly.

"The one to the left," Wilton answering, stepping to the table with a questioning look.

Holmes sighed and nodded, and the old man pulled back the dirty sheet.

Like most strangulation victims, the woman's face was swollen and mottled. Beyond the colour of her hair, I could not make out any features of her face. Time had not hardened me to the sight. Holmes and I both flinched in sympathy. She was stripped but clearly had not yet been washed. Holmes, as usual, was pleased.

"Perfect," Holmes said as if talking to himself.

He started with the ligature at her neck, using his magnifying glass to peer closely at the marks. "This was done by a rope," he murmured. He sucked in a surprised breath and straightened. "Wire rope, to be more specific."

He stood and looked back at the box of deceased man's effects, a small frown creasing his wide brow.

"Wait a moment, what are you suggesting?" I asked.

"I suggest nothing. This is a fact."

He retrieved the rope from the box without asking permission and spent some time with his magnifying glass at the woman's neck, comparing the wound to the material. Wilton and I waited patiently.

"This is not the same rope, obviously, but the same type was clearly used to kill both our mystery man and Agatha's mother," he said at last, straightening. His tone was flat, purposefully emotionless.

"Does it mean that this murder and our unknown sailor are connected?"

He clucked his tongue thoughtfully but didn't answer, scurrying down and examining the rest of the body.

"There is evidence here of some torture. I suspect she did not give them something they wanted, and they killed her in anger," he declared.

"What signs of torture?" I asked, horrified.

"Her fingers were broken, and there are bruises on her sternum and around her shoulders. Hullo, what is this?"

He was looking closely are her bare wrist. I stepped close to peep over his shoulder. "See here?" he said, "these scratches." A series of vertical, haphazard scratches, red and angry, marred her wrists and hands.

"More torture?" I asked.

Holmes looked unconvinced. He continued downwards until he reached her legs, making another exclamation of discovery. "They are here too, limited to a very specific horizontal band around her lower leg." He leaned back, resting his arm on his knee and thinking. "Doctor, correct me if I am wrong, but this area of the leg is roughly where a woman's socks would end but before the cuff of her pantaloons? Protected only by a layer of stocking?"

"Yes, I'd guess that could be true."

"Well, I've found all I can here." He covered the body once more with the sheet.

The first tendrils of sunset were reaching across the sky when we exited. We had put some distance between us and the mortuary before Holmes stopped on the kerb at the crossing of Church Street and spent some time tapping his knuckles against his chin, his expression far off, deep in thought. I waited patiently until he came back to himself with a large, frankly dramatic sigh, and signaled for a passing cab.

"Get in, Watson," he ordered as the driver slowed next to us.

"Where are we going?"

"I said get in," he repeated crossly. He turned to the driver. "Take us to 34 Harley Street."

When he turned back, he shook his head at my smirk. "Not a word, doctor. Not a word."

Harley Street was familiar to me. Though I had lived in Paddington when I was in practice, the sight of the rooms – likely filled with happily married medical men much like myself, once upon a time - caused a slight pang of grief as I was reminded of the small flat I had shared with Mary before her tragic death and my return to Baker Street. I wondered who resided in our old rooms, living their everyday lives within the walls of our comfortable home where we had eaten together, read together, slept together.

Holmes drew me from my thoughts with a soft tap against my knee. "Are you all right, doctor?" he asked gently.

I nodded. "Merely reminiscing."

He hummed sympathetically.

"You know how it is to look back on those meaningful moments with the woman you loved," I continued.

He gave me a surprised, suspicious look before he realized I was teasing him. He sighed. "It's not amusing, doctor."

I shrugged. "I suppose it's not, but that doesn't mean I can't find some humour in your embarrassment."

"Ah, the mark of true friendship."

I laughed. "Actually, yes."

Thirty-four Harley Street was a modest size, two-story house that spoke of admirable success but not extreme wealth. The three steps leading to the doorway were recently white-washed, and the flower boxes in the windows were carefully tended to.

The door was answered by a pleasant butler who seemed not at all surprised by our request to see Agatha. We were let into an airy sitting-room and asked to wait. I suppose I shouldn't have been astonished when it was not Agatha who entered the room a few minutes later but, rather, a handsome man of about 40 years.

He closed the door and immediately approached Holmes, holding out his hand. "Dr. Chambers, sir. I presume you're Mr. Holmes. The illustrations in The Strand are hardly accurate, but I judge from the lack of a mustache that you are the detective." He shook my friend's hand before shaking mine. "And you are the doctor and biographer. An absolute pleasure to meet both you gentlemen. You're one of the few men whose renown, I believe, is actually earned."

Holmes took this praise with modest appreciation; as he had gotten older, he had become more inured to the praise that was often heaped upon him, both sincere and insincere.

"I wondered if you would meet us," my friend remarked. "Agatha's description of you was one of a man admirably protective."

A flicker of a frown crossed the doctor's face at Holmes's use of the maid's first name, but his expression cleared when Holmes explained that Miss Davis had asked us to look into her mother's death and her subsequent attempted kidnapping.

"I can confirm her telling of events," said the man, "I heard her screaming last night, and when I opened the door, she was running up the street. I thought I saw two men behind her, but by the time she was safely inside, they were gone. I went out to look around, but they must have realized that this area is not one wherein thugs can simply carry off a struggling woman without notice."

"It seems too coincidental that this attack on her came so close on the heels of her mother's murder. I'd like to look into it, if I can speak to her and get her mother's address."

"Of course. I feel much relieved that she has more able-bodied men on her side to keep her safe. I'll ask Paxton to fetch her." As he went to the door to call for the butler, I cast Holmes an amused glance; it was clear this man's affection for Miss Davis went much deeper than merely a protective employer.

Agatha rushed into the room in a flurry of emotion. She went straight away to Holmes, grasping at his hands and thanking him profusely for deigning to help her. Holmes took her attentions with aplomb but looked immensely relieved when Dr. Chambers gently removed her.

"I can't express how happy I am that you are going to help me find out what happened to my mum!" she exclaimed, her eyes wet.

Holmes, a safe distance away, nodded. "All I require, miss, is the address of your mother's flat."

"Oh!" she exclaimed, "I'll bring you there! Allow me to put on my shawl." She hurried from the room before Holmes could protest.

"You have no objection to her accompanying us?" Holmes asked Chambers. I suspected he was hopeful the man would object and deter her, but the doctor nodded.

"I see no problem. I don't worry for her safety in the company of two men such as yourself. I trust you will not allow her to be snatched away."

"All right then," Holmes muttered, resigned.

We fetched a four-wheeler, and my friend said nothing as the girl sat next to him on the bench chair, oblivious to his discomfort.

I took pity on him and asked her questions about her mother. This prompted a steady stream of speech that spoke of her grief but also her ease with words. I remembered Holmes making an off-hand jest about his long talks with the maid while masquerading as that rakish plumber and understood what he meant. I found it endearing, however. She was a sweet woman and her voice was pleasing. I couldn't imagine that Holmes had really been that put out by her company.

Her mother had lived in a makeshift flat off a dim and dreary alley on Dorset Street. A few police still remained loitering about, and we were stopped at the doorway by a man who introduced himself, quite rudely, as Inspector Matheson. When we explained our business, he scoffed.

"Not much to see but the messy room of an old dead crone. One of many around here. She must have gotten on the bad side of her latest bully."

"Sir," I admonished, horrified by such speech in front of a woman, and the victim's daughter, no less.

Agatha, though pale-faced at her mother being spoken of in this way, seemed unsurprised by the inspector's attitude.

"We only wish to look around," Holmes ground out. "Surely, if as you say it is a commonplace murder, then no harm can come from our examination."

The man hesitated but shrugged, "I have no objection, but the landlady is coming to clean out all the bric-a-brac and rubbish as soon as the inspector arrives and gives her permission, so you best hurry."

Holmes didn't waste time continuing the conversation. He pushed past the man and into the small flat, eager to start his examination as quickly as possible.

The room was square, barely the size of our sitting-room with a layer of old mattresses in the corner, blanketed carefully in a way that spoke of a woman trying to make the best of her situation. The rest of the room was occupied by a water basin, a stove, and a few bookshelves with old books that appeared to be fished from the trash.

Agatha noticed my observation. "My mum wasn't a good reader, but she enjoyed it. She made sure my uncle gave me a good education in reading and writing. She said it was the pathway to a better life." Her eyes were wet, but she laughed at a sudden memory. "She gave one doctor a tongue lashing when he told her that reading led a woman to being unable to have children – an idea that Dr. Chambers, thankfully, strongly disagrees with." She gave me a questioning look.

"It is a ridiculous notion," I confirmed. She nodded. I felt strangely pleased as if I had just passed some sort of test.

She glanced around her mother's rooms and swallowed thickly. "Pardon me, sirs, but I think I'll step outside. Please call me if you think I could be of some help."

Holmes and I nodded sympathetically, and it was only after the crooked door had closed behind her that Holmes sprang into action, darting to and fro seemingly at random to different corners in the small room. At one point, he stood for some time staring at the small wallet portrait of Agatha that had seemingly fluttered to the ground near the water basin as if in deep thought before he dropped to the ground with his magnifying glass and, with most intense concentration, examined every scratch and mark on the old unvarnished wood. His face showed that his quest was not a successful one.

I leaned down over the picture that had captured his attention before, peering at the faded, smiling face of a much younger Agatha and wondered at the unfairness of such a sweet girl being born into such disadvantaged circumstances.

I saw nothing else in that sepia visage that could have been of note to the crime, so I stood and looked around. It was clear that the tiny flat had been rummaged through. The woman's books and clothes were scattered around. I guessed the search was both quick and fruitless.

"They were looking for something, Holmes."

He grunted. "Yes, likely whatever it is they were interrogating her about." He took the two steps that centered him in the room and pocketed his magnifying glass. "There were two of them. Both sailors. One has a slight limp and shoes that are somewhat too large for him. They used rope to secure her and spent some time roughing her up before strangling her which, I suspect, was due to a fit of anger and not part of a premeditated plan. They saw the picture of Agatha and made some connection. How they discovered her name or whereabouts, I'm not sure. I can hardly believe her mother would endanger her. If she was so hell-bent in staying silent that she was willing to die, I'm sure she would not have divulged details of her daughter that would put her in harm's way."

Agatha stepped in. "The inspector is coming down the alley, sir," she warned us with a waver in her voice.

Holmes sprung to his feet and began a harried examination of the room, clearly adverse to bandying words with another doltish member of the official police force. It was helpful that the space was so small. He paused at the fireplace, digging around in the ashes and pulling out a charred remnant of paper. He held it up to the light, but no words could be seen.

"Do you think the killers burned this?"

"Difficult to know." He glanced around until he found a small pocket-sized book and carefully slipped the brittle paper into the pages and placed it into his pocket for safekeeping.

"Are you able to see what is written on there?" Agatha asked.

"There may be some way to expose the writing," Holmes said, "but it is not guaranteed."

The inspector and the landlady entered then and brusquely rushed us out of the room. Holmes went with no protestation only because he had found everything he could discover.

Once back on Dorset Street, Agatha took desperate hold of Holmes's arm. "What did you see, Mr. Holmes? Do you know why someone would do such a thing to mum? There could be no reason to hurt her. As you saw, she had nothing. She meant nothing to anyone except to me."

Holmes gently disentangled himself. "I know nothing for sure. Allow me to work on this note. For now, we'll escort you back to your home to make sure you're safe under the benevolent watch of Dr. Chambers."

If the sniffling housemaid noticed the slight humour behind Holmes's use of the word *benevolent*, she did not make any outward show of it. I handed her my handkerchief as Holmes flagged down a passing cab, and we bustled in.

Agatha fell into a sad reverie, staring out of the cab's window. It was clear that brief glimpse of her mother's rummaged flat had affected her deeply. Once the strained air in the carriage became overpowering, I felt it my duty to distract her from her thoughts.

I directed my question to the detective, "Once a paper is burned, Holmes, I was under the impression it was impossible to recover what it contained."

"Difficult but not impossible," he answered. "There has been success with an alcohol and glycerin solution, diluted with water. When you place the charred item into the solution, as it immerses, decipherment can be made to varying degrees."

Agatha sniffed and used the edge of my pocket square to wipe at her eyes. "Do you think my mum burned the paper or her killers?"

"Likely your mother in order to hide whatever it is the intruders were after."

"What could have been so important that she would die for?"

Holmes's face softened with something startlingly close to affection. "You?" he suggested softly.

She looked very stunned by his words. "You believe my mum died to protect me?"

"It seems an obvious fact. Forgive me for my bluntness, but as you yourself already said, your mother did not have anything that seemed of any worth – except you. And there was an attempt to kidnap you very soon after her death."

"She never spoke of anything."

"It may have been a recent development. When did you last speak to your mother?"

"Last Saturday when I went home to visit."

We arrived at the front of Chambers' door on the peaceful Harley Street. Holmes disembarked the cab and offered his hand to the girl to help her down.

"Did your mother have any meaningful or extensive connection to sailors?" he asked as he knocked on Chambers' door.

Agatha frowned. "No, I don't think so. Of course, Whitechapel is an odd place and one often finds themselves in strange company. To be truthful. I only really have memories of her after my uncle died and I went back to live with her, but by that time, she kept mostly to herself. She wasn't one to socialize with anyone besides me."

"And why was that?"

"Because I'm a joy to be around," she replied smartly, a charming cleverness escaping even through her sniffles and tears.

Holmes hadn't been expecting the remark. He laughed one of his rare bright laughs, that pleasant smile stretching across his face and serving to make him look as young as when I first met him.

Agatha visibly started, glancing at him quickly and then glancing again, a sudden look of recognition unfolding on her open face. I understood immediately what had just transpired, and a part of me wondered why it had taken so long. I felt myself tense, though I was not yet sure to whose defense I was preparing to come.

Holmes understood the moment as well. His stance became guarded, as readying himself for a blow.

We held our breath.

It didn't come.

Agatha stared for a long while, a sad look of disappointment marring her pretty face, and then the door opened, the warm light of the small foyer falling over her as Paxton allowed her entry.

She stepped in with a quiet goodbye.

Holmes was understandably subdued as we rode back to Baker Street. I didn't know what to say. My amusement at the entire debacle had faded now that I had seen that look of pitiful betrayal on the innocent girl's face.

As we neared our flat, I opened my mouth to offer some reassuring counsel, but Holmes shot me such a withering glare of forewarning that the words died on my tongue.

We ascended the stairs in tense silence. Upon entering our comfortably messy flat, Holmes hung up his coats and went straight away to his chemical desk, rummaging around the bottles and vials.

"Will you fetch me about a liter of water, Watson?"

When I brought the pitcher back up, Holmes had filled a small photo development tray with alcohol and glycerin. He took the water from me without thanks and poured some into the mixture. He did not seem to be amenable to my company, so I took a seat and waited as he let the small piece of paper sink into the tray.

He hummed under his breath and used a spare piece of paper from his desk to write down the letters that appeared. He took his time with it and was still writing long after the paper had sunk to the bottom and began to turn to mush.

I could not tell if the tightness of his shoulders was due to some failure of the test or the situation with our client, though I guessed it was the latter by the amount of writing he was absorbed in.

"You can't be too surprised, Holmes," I ventured carefully.

He scoffed, still bent at his task. "I'm not surprised. This is precisely why I wanted to turn her away."

"Perhaps this will work out in the end. It will offer you an opportunity to explain. Apologize."

"I'm sure that will make everything all right," he sneered.

"It could at least reassure her that Escott's disappearance was due to no fault on her part."

"I'm no expert at women, Watson, but I don't think that will dull the sting."

Considering how quickly he had secured her hand in betrothal, I had my doubts that his knowledge of women was really as lacking as he professed. "She seems a forgiving sort-"

"I used her."

I was shocked at the admission. "For a noble cause," I offered.

"Again, the sting, Watson."

I sighed. "A frank talk with her may be inevitable, Holmes. Unless you intend to abandon this case."

"I will do nothing of the sort. In fact-" he passed the scrap of paper to me where he had been attempting to make sense of the few letters his experiment managed to reveal. "I believe I have the first sentence of this letter – the best I could manage."

The sentence he uncovered was a simple but significant *Agatha dear, I have in my posses-*. The proceeding letters were lost forever, but it did not take a world-renowned intellect to know what it said.

"A shame we can't read the rest to know what she had in her possession that she was willing to die for. Or if it was found."

Holmes shook his head, "It was not found. If they had what they wanted, why would they risk taking Agatha in the middle of a well to-do street? And we still do not have answers as to how this murder may be linked to the sailor left hanging in a very purposeful public display."

He disappeared into his room and emerged about an hour later dressed as a rough sailor and told me not to wait up for his return.

The evening was young, and I felt suddenly adrift. I could smell Mrs. Hudson cooking the lamb shanks I had spied when I went down to the kitchen to collect the water. The clock ticked by a few minutes as I sat and wondered how to spend my time, an increasingly common occurrence for me. In moments like these, I considered the wisdom of perhaps opening my own practice once again.

But that was hardly something I could do immediately. I shook myself. My publisher wanted my first draft of the Baskerville adventure, and I remembered that I had lent the notes to Holmes to get his comments. I poked around his desk, looking for my papers. I opened the top drawer and instead came upon copious documents he had written on beekeeping, of all things. I stood staring sort of dumbly at them for a long while. It was not that I was unaware of Holmes's interest; indeed, he had spoken many times of his thoughts on the matter of apiology, but I did not know he had made so much formal inquiry into it or written so very much.

I felt a pang of grief hit me. I had long suspected that Holmes was considering retirement. He was not old, in January he had turned 47 years of age and was still healthy and physically strong, but these last ten years or so had carried with them a sort of deep melancholy that was different than his youthful tendency to brood. His mind was as sharp as ever, and his love for his work had not waned, but it seemed his desire to be flush with the world had diminished. More and more, he sought out solitude and quiet, and I feared soon he may do so in a manner more permanent. And where would that leave me?

I set the bundle down carefully and found my own notes that I had been looking for. Holmes had written quick, helpful comments in the margins in that unique shorthand he used that I could now read like a second language.

I pushed all other thoughts from my mind and settled comfortably in my armchair to read through his edits on our harrowing adventure in Dartmouth.

Holmes did not return until late the next morning. He was rubbing tiredly at his eyes and disappeared into his room without a word. I heard his wardrobe opening and closing and then his movement in the washroom.

He emerged clean and dressed in his favorite dressing gown. His eyes were still lined with exhaustion. I kindly pushed a plate of eggs and rashers in his direction. "Long night?" I ventured.

He poured a cup of tea from the cooling teapot and downed it without complaint. "If you ever visit the Drunken Mermaid pub, Watson, I advise you to steer clear of their housemade gin. Vile stuff."

"You spent the entire night at the pub?"

"Part of it in a room behind the bar as I didn't trust myself to walk." He ate a few bites of his eggs and then moved them away with a grimace.

He turned his attention once again to the tea. "I stationed myself there," said he, "to see if I could find any information about our dead man. It's a popular stop for sailors who have recently gotten into port. It took some time, and an unfortunate amount of gin, before I stumbled upon anything of interest."

"Care to share?"

He stood and filled his after-breakfast pipe. "The day before our sailor was found dead, a commercial fishing ship *The Seafarer* docked in port, cutting their expedition short because they lost their captain at sea. A group of garrulous and quite drunk men told me that one of the men on the ship's log frequents the pub, a Mark Ingels. They then tried to ply me with absinthe which I declined in favor of my healthy liver. I managed, I hope, to write out a note to this Ingels before the proprietor allowed me to sleep off my inebriation in the back room. If my note was legible, I expect a visit from the man sometime this afternoon." He shook his head ruefully. "I'm getting old, dear doctor. A little over-indulgence in spirits wouldn't have sent me under the table when I was 30."

"Why would they try to ply you with absinthe?"

He shrugged. "They found it amusing. I wasn't familiar with the establishment and thus did not realize what a weathered crowd usually gathered there. Even in my rough attire, I evidently stood out." He grimaced. "They called me 'pretty boy' and bought me the first few rounds of gin to see how well I fared. I handled it admirably, if I do say so myself, but around the sixth shot, even I couldn't pretend to be unaffected."

I laughed. "I hardly think you could be described as a 'boy' anymore."

He glared. Indeed, Holmes had aged well with only the beginnings of a frustratingly becoming grey appearing in his black hair and the whiskers on his face, which he had not yet shaved after his long night, but he was clearly no youth.

He cocked his head in the direction of the stairs. "If I'm not mistaken, there is our man now."

The door opened and the page showed in a small ribston-pippin of a man with a jovial smile and a twinkle in his eye that spoke of a good-natured disposition.

"'Ello there," he greeted us, "Old onion breath at the Mermaid said you were looking for me."

"I beg your pardon?" I stuttered.

Holmes just laughed, bidding the man to sit. "He means the pub owner, Watson. An affectionate – and apt – nickname."

"From what I could make of your note, you wish to speak to me of our last voyage." He held the note out, and Holmes took it. At the sight of his own unsteady handwriting, he grimaced.

"Yes. You're Mark Ingels, correct?"

"Yes, sir. A fisherman on *The Seafarer*. Our last trip had proven unusual, so I'm not too surprised it has become the topic of interest."

"Can you describe what about this trip was eventful?"

"Actually, in some ways it was very uneventful – we hardly caught anything. We were barely out at sea two days before the captain fell ill. His breathing was all wet, and then on the third day he died. That's why we returned so early and empty-handed."

"What was your captain's name?"

"Pattins."

"And what became of his body?"

"He was taken to the morgue and then buried. I was there with his wife."

Holmes frowned in disappointment.

The man recognized the expression. "I beg your pardon, sir, but are you looking for someone?"

"Did you hear of the man who was hung at the London hospital?"

"Aye, I heard tale of it, but I don't know much about it. And I certainly had nothing to do with it."

"He was a sailor."

"Was he?" the man murmured curiously. "Do you have reason to think he was on my boat?"

"Has anyone gone missing?"

He waved his hand helplessly. "Most of us don't keep in company with each other while on land. We see enough of each other on that cramped ship. Though ..." he trailed off thoughtfully.

"Yes?" Holmes prompted with an edge of impatience.

"Jack Harper was acting sort of odd when we docked."

"Who is he?"

"First mate. He was very close to Pattins. I think they'd been working together for about 10 years now. In fact, he spent the day with him in his cabin when he fell ill."

"And this struck you as suspicious?"

"Not at all, but once we reached land, Jack was acting real skittish. He ran off, didn't even show up when Pattins was buried. Me and him got on just fine, better than fine, in fact, but he avoided me when he would normally spend some time with me at the pubs or go to a little peep show-" he broke off, eyes widening upon remembering that he was not speaking to fellow sailors. "What I mean is-"

"It's all right," Holmes waved away, eager to get on with it. "Continue."

"Anyhoo, as I said, he scurried right off. I caught a glimpse of him later that night when I was at The Raven and Rat. He was going into Mrs. Miller's inn across the street. I waved, but he darted into the building as if he didn't want to be seen."

"What does Jack Harper look like?"

"Sandy hair. Short at about five and half feet tall. A stocky man. Do you think he was the man who was killed?"

"He fits the description," Holmes answered bluntly.

"Damn man," Ingels swore, "Why wouldn't he tell me what he had gotten into?"

"Did he appear to be in possession of a box or any item that he did not have when he boarded the ship?"

"No, just his ditty bag."

Holmes stared into the cold fireplace for a while before nodding. "You said Mrs. Miller's inn on Red Lion Street?"

"Yes, sir."

Holmes stood and thanked the man. "I'm endeavoring to discover what happened to your friend. I'll send you word at the Mermaid when I have information. Do you expect to be in London for long?"

"I have no plans, as of yet, though my empty pockets will eventually compel me to find a position on board another boat."

"Well, then, let's hope I am quick about it."

Once he was gone, Holmes tossed off his dressing-gown. "I think a trip to Harper's rooms are in order. Would you care to join me?"

As we rode again to Whitechapel, I broached the topic of Agatha once more. "You know, Holmes, once we discover the truth of this mystery, you will have to face the girl again."

Surprisingly, he didn't appear annoyed by my statement. He sighed. "I'm aware, Watson. In fact, it occurs to me that our housemaid is very intelligent and has likely drawn the connection between her erstwhile fiancée's disappearance and the death of her employer. The connection she may draw, however, may put us in a rough spot if she presumes we had some hand in his death."

"It would be unfortunate if she made a trip to Scotland Yard to turn us in," I said.

"I'm sure that would please Lestrade, but I've avoided a gaol cell – for the most part – thus far, and I have no intention of ending my illustrious career by being collared by the nitwits of the Metropolitan Police Force."

"You mustn't try to defend yourself when you speak to her," I advised, "Let her talk and listen."

"I know how to converse with people, doctor."

"Not when you are so clearly in the wrong."

He grunted at that and took to watching the scenery move by as we descended into the spider web streets of the East End.

Mrs. Miller's inn was a depressing two-story rectangle building bracketed by a pawnshop on the left and a small alley leading to the back yard. Holmes did not immediately approach the entrance but instead gestured to the alley.

"I wish to see if there is any evidence of illegal entrance," he told me as we squeezed through the broken iron fence that led to the barren strip of dried grass that constituted the back yard. Center-right of the building was a sturdy but leafless tree with spindly branches that looked as if it would have been luxurious with proper tending-to. Its grey arms spread out across the first-story windows of the inn. Holmes pointed upwards.

"See that window? Its glass is broken."

One of the windows near the middle did have a broken window pane. Holmes went to stand beneath it, staring at the pathway of the tree.

"It looks as if someone climbed here and broke the glass to unlock the window," he suggested. He touched the tree bark and then hefted himself up by one low hanging branch to test his theory. It held his weight, but he hissed and dropped back down, looking at his palm.

"Rough," he commented, showing me the scratches on his palm. "Look familiar?"

They looked identical to the marks we had seen on Agatha's mother. "Do you think she broke the window pane?"

"Either she broke it, or simply used the fact that someone else broke it in order to enter. Come, let us see if Mrs. Miller will allow us to peruse her former tenant's room."

Mrs. Miller was cooperative once Holmes handed over a few shillings. She told us that Harper had vanished a few days ago, but he had paid a week in advance and his things were still there. She left us to find the place ourselves, and we ascended the dark, creaking staircase to a hallway lined with yellowing wallpaper.

Like most inns of this sort, Harper's room was a square space with a cot. A basin with questionable water stood on an uneven little table in one corner. The grimy covers and sheets were in disarray, as if someone had ripped them from the bed. The only item of Harper's present was his sailor's cloth bag crumpled on the ground, its contents poured from them. His extra clothes, sewing kit, a few books, and assorted toiletries were strewn around the room.

"Someone was looking for something," I commented.

"Astute observation. But did they find it? I think not, since they strung him up."

"But how would that help?"

"By sending a message to whoever *was* in possession of the valuables they were after."

"Evidently Miss Agatha's mother did not get the message."

Holmes shook his head, sitting thoughtfully on the bed. "I think she did. I believe that is why they were unable to find the item - or items - on her. She must have hid her treasure once she knew it was at risk."

"There was no place to hide it in her little flat, Holmes. Perhaps Agatha knows of some of her mother's common haunts, places where she could secret items away temporarily."

Holmes shook his head again. "I think the answer is much simpler. From the scratches on her hands and legs, we can presume she came here, entering through the window. Perhaps following the path of our killers."

"But why would she follow them? Do you think she was investigating them in some way?"

"No, I believe she came here for a much more ingenious reason. Where is the perfect place to hide something that you know others have been looking for?"

I had to think a second before it became obvious. "You believe she returned here and hid the item because she knew they would not return to a place they had already searched?"

"Clever, hmmm?"

He stood and lifted the flat mattress. Finding nothing, he began to shake out the bedding. I looked in Harper's discarded bag and then picked up one of the well-worn books. I chuckled at the title. *Moby Dick*.

I ruffled through the novel and then felt my mouth fall open in shock. I stared mutely down at the papers that had been stuffed in the pages of the book.

"Holmes," I started, "I believe I found what we're looking for." I looked up as he took the two strides that brought him next to me. "Bearer bonds," I explained, removing them and letting the book drop to the ground. "Nearly 1000 pounds worth of bearer bonds."

Holmes snatched some of them from me in excitement. "That'll do it," he murmured gleefully. "I wonder if Harper stole these from his dead captain."

"There's a letter here," I pointed out, showing him the small note handwritten on a cheap piece of paper. We read it together:

> *Dear Alice,*
>
> *I cannot tell you how happy I was to see you last. The few days we spent together reminded me of when we were young and so ignorantly in love. I have always loved you, even after all these years. I understand why you did not tell me of Agatha. It stung to know you had kept my daughter from me, but when you explained you were only trying to avoid making me feel obligated, I knew you were a kind-hearted woman. Too kind, though. I would not have felt trapped. I would have done whatever I could to know her, care for her. I missed so much of her life, but from what you told me, she is a lovely, smart girl. And she knows how to read and write! My love, I cannot thank you enough for that blessing.*
>
> *I have the means to repay you for all you have struggled alone. My captain and friend fell very ill very suddenly on our last voyage. I*

stayed with him until his final breath. He was a simple man, at home at the sea, with no remaining family. As it became clear he was not long for this world, he told me a great secret. His grandfather, before he died, had passed onto him wealth in the form of bonds worth 980 pounds. Pattins – that was my friend's name – had no use for it. His home was The Seafarer, his happiness the sea. He kept the notes in his safe, unsure what to do with them and possessing no kin to which to pass them. As he lay dying, he had me unlock this safe and told me to take them - that I had served him well and been like a son to him.

I cannot tell you what a shock it was to have such wealth in my grasp. I instantly thought of Agatha, of you, and how I could save both of you from a life of dreadful servitude to others.

The day's journey back to land after his death were harrowing. I had to keep the bonds on me and knew that I could find myself in the depths of the sea if the other men discovered what I possessed. Two of them, Watkins and Quill, seemed suspicious. I hardly know how they could have learned of the bonds, perhaps the scoundrels were listening in somehow, but in any case, I sensed they were watching me. I am trying to stay out of sight, but I fear they may be on my heels.

I'm giving you the bonds. Please pass them to Agatha – I know she is safe with that fancy doctor of hers. Once I feel I am not being shadowed any longer, I will come to you. I wish to meet my daughter and be a part of her life. I wish to be a part of yours as well, but I will leave that decision up to you.

Be on guard.

All my love,
Jack

"I hardly think the man would have guessed all this would lead to his death as well as the death of the mother of his child," Holmes said sadly. "The gross injustices people will commit for a little bit of money will never cease to dismay me."

"You realize," I pointed out, "That two people have died for these and now we have them in our hands?"

Holmes plucked the letter from my grasp, folding it in with the bearer bonds and tucking the bundle into his pocket.

"I'm aware of that perilous fact," he said with entirely too much liveliness in his voice. "So I think it in our best interest to remove ourselves to Harley Street as soon as possible. I can send one of my Irregulars to Scotland Yard with the name of our two men, as well as directions to find Mark Ingels so he may provide a description. You have your revolver with you?"

"No, I do not," I answered testily. "I don't carry a firearm everywhere."

He tsked. "No worries, I have my trusted walking stick and its secret blade, but I don't think we will be molested. The men have no reason to have eyes on this room now that they've killed Harper."

Holmes was correct, and we managed our journey with no dastardly interference. I had no doubt the house on Harley Street was being watched, our ruthless murderers on the lookout for any opportunity to grab the girl again. I shuddered to think of Agatha in the hands of men who were not above torturing a woman. The quicker she cashed these bonds and secured the funds as hers, the quicker she would be out of harm's way.

Paxton once again let us in what that solemnity that seemed out of place on his relatively youthful face. We waited in the sitting-room until Chambers entered and greeted us. An extremely fluffy calico cat followed him in, curling up on the divan like a queen.

"I'm so pleased to see you," he said, shaking our hands vigorously. "I hope you have news. I canceled all my patients today so as not to leave Agatha alone. Paxton is a hardy fellow, but two men is better than one, and I would not have been able to concentrate on my work separated and unsure of what was happening."

I held back a smile, wondering if he knew how obvious his feelings were.

"We have plunged to the heart of the matter," Holmes reassured. "I can answer all her questions and furnish her a pleasant surprise, if she will see me."

I understood the implication, but Chambers merely nodded and made haste to fetch her. I was thankful she had clearly kept her revelations about Holmes to herself, another mark of her fine character.

When the doctor returned with her, she entered with much more reserve than usual. She clasped her hands and nodded stiffly avoiding direct eye contact with either of us.

"Sirs," was all she said in greeting.

Holmes seemed unsure how to proceed for a moment. Glancing at Chambers, he chose to ignore the elephant in the room and barreled through with the mystery at hand.

"Miss Davis," he started, voice patently matter-of-fact, "I'm happy to tell you that we have discovered the motive for your mother's murder." He gave her a succinct overview of Harper's account, leaving out the letter or any reference to Agatha's mother.

"You see," he finished, "his captain had passed on a sort of inheritance, but the nature of the bearer bonds, being so similar to cash, put him in a perilous position. It is why he was killed and hung so publicly. You heard of this in the paper?"

She frowned. "I did, but I'm not sure why this story would interest me, frankly. Did you come here to brag of another case you solved instead of my mother's?"

Holmes visibly recoiled at the venom in her words. "No," he assured softly, "The two events are connected. Forgive my lack of brevity. Perhaps Jack Harper can explain better than I can." He removed the letter and with a careful air of respect passed it to her.

We all waited as she read, watching her face transform from confusion to shock. Long after I knew she was finished reading, she stared down at the words with a distant look in her eye.

At last, she raised her head and peered intently at Holmes. "So my mum did die for me? She was so desperate that I receive this gift that she refused to tell them where it was?"

Holmes nodded. "Your father too. He did not know you, but as you can see, that did not dull his love for you. I know, if given a choice, you would trade these pieces of paper for your parents, but the knowledge that you were that cared for I hope provides some solace."

I handed her the bonds. Chambers looked over her shoulder, clearly interested in making sure they were authentic.

"I will get these transferred to an account at the Bank of England under her name," he assured us. "I'll make sure the money is secured so no one may access the funds but Agatha."

With unquestioning trust, Agatha handed the bonds to him. "And the men that killed my mum?" she asked.

"We know their names," Holmes explained, "and a shipmate of your father's can provide their descriptions. I will notify Scotland Yard immediately. We will secure the ports to be sure they cannot slip away on another ship." He paused as if unsure what else to say. Abruptly, he concluded, "You're a woman of some means now, Agatha. I sincerely wish you the best in your life."

He nodded at her, then at Chambers, turning to leave. I made to follow, but he stopped suddenly and turned, looking resigned. "Dr. Chambers, I know it may seem a bit improper, but would you allow me to speak to Miss Davis alone for a moment?"

The doctor looked surprised but nodded, evidently loathe to deny Holmes his request after the service he had provided. "You can step into the dining-room here," he pointed to an adjoining room.

Holmes glanced at Agatha for permission. I thought she would refuse, but she went willingly into the next room. Holmes closed the door, leaving the doctor and me standing in confused silence.

"Do you know what that's about?" he asked me bluntly after some time had passed.

"I suspect I do," I admitted, "but it is not my place to say anything."

"I see."

"Speaking of not my place," I began hesitantly, "I hope you'll forgive my forwardness, but Agatha's station in life has just made a turn for the better. Perhaps her circumstances may change in another area as well?" I suggested.

He reddened. "I was that obvious? Well, no need to urge me, Dr.

Watson. I have been considering it for some time. I'm not the boldest or most confident of men when it comes to things of that sort."

"I think you may be confident. I do have some experience in this, and I believe she reciprocates your feelings."

He looked relieved, but merely nodded.

The door to the dining-room opened and our two companions emerged. The air was not antagonistic, though Holmes was a bit flush. He jerked his chin down in a quick goodbye to our host, beckoning me to follow.

"Thank you, Mr. Holmes. You as well, Dr. Watson," Agatha said softly to our backs. I hesitate to say it was forgiveness I heard in her voice, but something close to it. I turned and bid her adieu, pleased at the look of gentleness on her face.

As we regained the kerb, I asked Holmes what he had said to her.

"What needed to be said, Watson," he replied curtly, "and that's all you'll ever know. Now come along. I have a sudden need for my pipe and some peace and quiet."

"But its effects are so deleterious, Holmes!" I declared, fighting the urge to toss my morning paper aside in anger. "I don't care if it is legal or not. I would say the same if someone engaged in an excess of alcohol."

"Mmmm, understandable," my flatmate murmured from his spot reclining on the divan in his blue dressing gown. His sleeve was still rolled up, and the syringe lay discarded carelessly next to his open morocco case.

"Holmes, you aren't listening to me."

"I am, doctor. I merely disagree."

"As a medical man, I think I would know more than you on the topic."

"Is that what you would think?"

The words were spoken with such amused condescension that I did throw my paper down onto the breakfast table in a fit of exasperation.

It was the warm summer of 1882. At the time, this personal habit of his was new to me. In the first year of our living arrangement, I had described my fellow lodger as possessing a 'temperance and cleanliness' that forbid the notion of narcotic usage. As we settled more comfortably in our lives together, I had recently discovered I was regrettably mistaken. Evidently, the man had simply been on his best behavior to avoid losing out on an agreeable arrangement with someone willing to split rent with him.

He looked at me through narrow eyes and sighed. "I assure you, Watson, I am fully in control of the dosage."

"I simply don't understand you, Holmes. Cocaine and morphine affect the mind – that great brain you take such pride in. It simply seems uncharacteristically foolhardy for you to dabble in such dangerous hobbies, at the risk of your carefully honed skills."

He let his head fall back and his eyes close. "That is exactly the point, old man. At times, it is pleasant to *not* think."

That gave me pause. I tried to place myself in my friend's shoes. I tried to imagine what it was like to see every small detail of the world as glaringly as I may see a glob of jam on a companion's face. It sounded tiring, but Holmes carried such pride in his deductive abilities that I found it surprising that he would express such a feeling.

"I'm a thoroughbred quivering at a gate that never opens," he continued, "There is no noteworthy crime to be seen. The lack of creativity in the criminal classes should, in and of itself, be a crime. Give me something worthy to occupy my mind, and the need for distraction vanishes." He waved his hand airily. I could see faded puncture marks on the pale underside of his arm.

I cast a dismayed glance around at the multitude of ruffled newspapers that dotted the sitting room. I fought with the urge to scour the pages for something to divert him, but I knew he had already gone over every word himself and found nothing to pique his interest.

We were saved by Mrs. Hudson's announcement that a young girl was waiting to see us. I sprang up, accepting the meeting before Holmes could respond, and hastily cleared up the paraphernalia scattered on the table.

Holmes, to his credit, stood, straightened his dressing gown, and sat in his chair, attempting to look presentable.

A diminutive girl roughly our age entered timidly. From the modest design of her dress, I gathered she was of the working class, perhaps a servant. She was not particularly pretty, but her face held a wide openness and an artistic scattering of freckles that was pleasing.

She waited for us to bid her to sit and did so as if commanded, solidifying my theory that she was employed in a household staff.

"I beg your pardons, sirs," she started, "I know I came without an appointment."

Holmes waved the apology aside. "I see that you are a parlor maid, and you arrived using your last coin on a carriage that you were obliged to disembark from some blocks away. You are recently engaged, but you have not yet informed your employers."

The girl glanced downwards at herself in surprise. After a moment, she frowned. "I can see how you might've guessed about the walking as I have some mud on my shoes, but I cannot see how you came about the rest, sir."

"Not just any mud but the specific color and consistency near the renovations of the apothecary nearby. The rest was similarly easy to deduce.

The direction you came from – as evidenced by the soil on your boots – would put you in the direction of Belgrave and Grosvenor Square. From the sturdiness of your boots, the slight fading of your well-mended bodice where your apron ties have rubbed over a period of time, and the slight wear at the knees of your skirt, I can easily deduce that you are a maid, specifically at one of the wealthier households as your clothes are of higher quality to reflect the station of your employers. I know you hired a carriage for at least part of your journey because your shoes hold traces of only one soil. Your coin purse is now empty, save for the faint impression of a ring inside that you wish to keep with you but secret."

She smiled with unabashed joy. "That's astonishing, sir. A few months ago, you helped the Newgates in a small matter. The lady's-maid there spoke highly of you. I'm glad she wasn't making up stories."

A slight flush crept up Holmes's cheeks at the praise. "A small matter, indeed. But I suspect something important weighs on you, dear."

"Well, yes. My name is Lucille, and I work as a parlor maid for a home on Chester Street. My employer, Mr. Philips, was murdered the day before last. It was in the papers." At this, she glanced around confusedly at the chaos of newsprint surrounding us.

"Yes, I recall it," Holmes answered. "His throat was slit in his parlor. They arrested the gardener."

"Asa," she clarified with some emotion in her voice. "His name is Asa, and I am sure he did not do it."

At the beat of silence and the quick glance Holmes and I shared, she frowned and shook her head vehemently. "I know what you think, sir, but this is not sentiment. As you said, I am spoken for. I've known Asa for years. His father was the gardener before he died, and Asa stayed on to take over his duties. I know him. What's more, there is no reason for him to kill Mr. Philips at all!"

Holmes sucked on the inside of his cheek for a moment before deciding to continue. "As of now, Miss Lucille, I'm not sure if your story merits further investigation, but I don't want to be hasty. Can you tell me exactly what events took place?"

"Of course. I was there when it happened. I didn't see the killing, thank God, but I saw his body." Here, her pleasant face was marred by the memory. "There was blood everywhere."

Holmes held up a hand. "A moment. I know it is tempting to jump straight away to the *plat de résistance*, but let's step back. Before that unpleasant event, what took place?"

"I was tending to the fireplace in the sitting room when I heard the dogs barking. The master has two Irish Setters that he dotes upon. Doted upon, rather," she corrected with a wince. "A few moments later, I heard some crashing and thudding noises from the parlor. I went to the door and called through, but there was no answer. I had no key, so I summoned the butler who was in the kitchen, and he unlocked the door." She took a moment to compose herself as if she were entering the room once more and needed to steel herself for the sight.

"Inside," she continued, "Mr. Philips was in his chair by the hearth with his throat slit. There was blood all down his front. Asa was standing next to him, and the patio door stood open."

"And his proximity to the body is what led to his arrest?"

"You mean was he collared only because he was near the body? Yes, I think so. Even he claimed he saw no one else enter or exit the parlor through the patio door."

"What doorways lead to the parlor?"

"Three, sir. The one I stood at opening to the hallway, the patio door leading to the backyard, and the door to the right to his study."

"Was the study searched?"

"Yes, no one else was there."

"Is there an exit from the study to the hallway?"

"Yes, but to flee out the front door, someone would have passed me and no one did. I am sure of it."

"The hallway provides no other means of egress?"

She faltered, clearly at a loss.

In a softer voice, Holmes rephrased, "There are no other doors connected to the hallway besides the study and parlor?"

"Oh! Well, the other wall of the hallway is shorter because the sitting room takes up the main space in the front. The parlor door is across that room under the stairway. The only other room opposite the parlor and connected study is the kitchen and servants' quarters."

"Is there a backdoor in the kitchen?"

"Of course, sir, but it has a basic latch that can only be locked from inside and the door was locked, so no one could have escaped through that way and secured the door behind them."

"Why is there only a latch?"

"There has always been an old latch, but the newer lock that we used to use broke a few months ago, and the master had yet to arrange for it to be fixed."

"What was the state of the parlor?"

"Some items on the master's desk were thrown about as if there was a struggle. The round table next to his chair where he put his teapot and cup were knocked over. That must have been the sounds I heard that so alarmed me."

"But he was in his chair by the fireplace?"

"Yes."

Holmes fell deep in thought for a long while as we waited patiently for him to reemerge. When he did, he leaned back and tapped his chin.

"Tell me about the family," he requested.

"Mr. Philips is a widower twice over. I only knew his last wife, a French woman by the name of Villiers, who died about seven years ago of something with her breathing," she struggled a bit to recall the name. "She got filled with water."

"Pneumonia," I supplied gently.

"Yes, I think that was it. She left behind a daughter named Adelaide. She is about twenty now. Mr. Philips also has an older son named Grant. He treated them both well, and he took care of Adelaide as if she was his own. He made his money making parts of steam engines, but he retired a few years ago."

"What is Adelaide like?"

"Very nice. Smart too. She never acts like she's better than us. Though I realize she is, of course," she corrected quickly. "In any case, she is a good person, and she has taken his death badly. I see her crying."

"And his son?"

"He keeps more of a distance but has never been unkind. To be honest, I do not know much about him."

"Do they both live in the house?"

"Yes."

"Where were they during the murder?"

"I don't really know where Adelaide was. After the chaos of finding Mr. Philips, she appeared. I guessed she came down from her room on the first floor. The other Mr. Philips, Grant, that is, had left for a play at the Princess Theater and did not return until later that night. Asa had been arrested, but the police were still there looking around when he returned."

"Who was the policeman in charge?"

She scrunched her face in strained recollection. "Gregory, I believe."

"Gregson, you mean?"

"Yes, that was it. He was nice. I don't think he really wanted to arrest Asa, but the boy was the only one there so it looks bad for him."

Holmes stood with a sudden burst of energy. "I'll look into this for you."

A huge sense of relief washed over me. I tried my best not to show it, but the young lady gave me a curious look. She stood as well. "Thank you so much, Mr. Holmes. I can't pay you much …"

"You needn't pay me at all," Holmes said brusquely. "If this proves interesting, that will be enough recompense. And I have no need to burden you with financial worries as I am aware of your situation. Now, here is some coin for your return. No, no, please take it. I cannot in good conscience send a lady off to make that journey by foot. I will arrange to meet Gregson at the house later today."

As soon as the brisk rustle of our charming guest's skirt had faded down the stairs, Holmes fetched Billy, sent off a short telegram to Gregson at Scotland Yard, and then retreated to his room, emerging half of an hour later fully dressed and immaculately groomed.

"Will you join me, Watson? I'm off to the Philips' to look around. We're meeting Gregson there."

"We have not yet received a reply from Gregson."

"I did not request one." He smoothed his hair in the looking glass above the mantle. "I directed him to meet us forthwith."

"And you simply assume that he will drop his other duties and responsibilities to obey your every whim?" I asked with amusement.

He lifted a dismissive shoulder. "Gregson is brighter than most of the other yard members combined. He won't choose to ignore further insights on a case."

Holmes was correct, of course. Gregson had preceded us there, and the alacrity with which he must have done so belied the annoyed protestation he greeted us with when we met him at the gate of the Philips' ornate, two-story Georgian home.

The blonde inspector tutted at us as he unlocked the wrought-iron gate and led us up the steps to the entrance.

"I'll never quite understand you, Holmes," said he, "you read a little entry in the newspaper about a murder and somehow see the complex mystery at the heart of it."

"While I would delight in permitting you to believe that of my powers of deduction, in this particular case, it is not true. A servant requested my help. You believe it is a complex case, Gregson?" Holmes probed.

"Its complexity lies in its lack of complexity, sir," the inspector sighed, unlocking the door and entering without knocking.

"Is the house empty, inspector?" I asked.

"No, the son and stepdaughter are still in residence, but the parlor and study are cordoned off and being watched by one of my men for the time being."

"May I ask why?" Holmes inquired with a certain amount of satisfaction in his voice, "I was under the impression that you had arrested the man?"

"I have arrested *a* man," Gregson corrected.

"Yes, a gardener by the name of Asa."

"Asa Andrews."

"Yet you seemed unconvinced of the rightness of this?"

We followed him into the foyer that branched off, on the right, to the spacious sitting room. Opposite, curved a beautiful wooden staircase, and under this was an asymmetrical hallway with three doors dotting the longer side and one door at the end of the short wall.

A young officer, who I vaguely remembered was called something like Williams or Willis, was leaning carelessly against the parlor door, straightening to attention as we entered.

"Well, Mr. Holmes," Gregson started, "the thing is, there really isn't any other answer for it. The young man was standing over the dead body moments after he was killed. There was no one else about."

"However?"

"I cannot figure the point. I've talked to the young man. He claims his innocence of course, and seems sincere. He gains nothing from his employer's death."

"Nothing that we are aware of, at least," Holmes suggested. "What story does he give?"

"He claims he heard the struggle as well and came in through the unlocked patio from the back garden. He says Mr. Philips was already dead."

"What was he doing outside?"

"Well, he's a gardener."

"Yes, but it was after dark."

"I'm not a gardener, Holmes."

Holmes gestured to the parlor door. "May I?"

Gregson opened the door. The parlor was a dimly lit area with a desk cluttered with papers; these were strewn about as if disturbed by a struggle. To the right, near the entrance to what I assumed was the study was a small fireplace bracketed by two comfy armchairs. The table next to it was toppled and the tray of tea and one lone teacup was scattered on the stone of the hearth.

The inspector apologized. "Of course, the body is gone and my men have been in and out of here. I have not moved anything else. I wasn't expecting you to come along," he added ruefully.

"Yes, yes, why preserve clues if I'm not here?" Holmes murmured sardonically, already examining the bloodstains on the armchair near the cold fireplace. "Ah, I assume this knife here is the murder weapon?" he pointed to a small porcelain-handled blade lying on the desk.

"Yes, I dusted it for fingerprints the best I knew how and there were none."

Holmes frowned at that, gently picking the weapon up with a gloved hand and analyzing it up close. He glanced back at the desk. "You observed, I'm sure, that this comes from Philips' set there?"

He pointed to a small glass case hanging open near the edge of the cabinet near the door.

"Of course." Gregson sighed. "At least that indicates a crime of passion. If this were planned, the murderer would not have needed to improvise in such a way."

"Hmmm," Holmes murmured with evident doubt. "The data could support multiple theories. It's always a mistake to become attached to one without properly excluding the others."

Properly chastened, Gregson quickly turned up the gaslight to allow Holmes to move about the space. We both stood and watched as he peered at almost every inch of the room with his magnifying glass and crawled around the carpet methodically and with complete disregard to the state of his own trousers.

When he was finished, he slipped his tool into his coat pocket and stood in the middle of the parlor, gazing around contemplatively.

"Was the gardener wearing gloves when you arrested him?"

Gregson's face filled with bright realization. "By Jove! He was not, Mr. Holmes."

"Then you're correct, Gregson. As is our bright parlor maid. There are multiple issues with the idea that dear Asa Andrews killed this man. One," he ticked off with long, scarred fingers, "there were sounds of a struggle, yet Philips seemed to be sitting in his chair when he died, his throat slit quickly.

Two, as you said, he had no gloves on, so why would the knife be bare of all fingerprints? And three, all Mr. Andrews would accomplish, as far as we know, by killing Mr. Philips is potentially making himself jobless. I assume this door leads to the patio and the backyard?" He pointed to the French doors and then strode through them without waiting for confirmation.

The patio was a midsized but elegant design of wood and awning. Three steps led down into the grassy yard lined with trees and meticulously maintained flowers. It was not large but was sufficient enough for some cozy benches and a gazebo nestled in the corner.

"The patio doors are not the only way to access the yard," Holmes noted, pointing at the narrow stone pathway that snaked beside one side of the house to a small gate opening to the shady alleyway.

"Correct, that's where the kitchen door opens as well," Gregson confirmed.

We followed Holmes as he sidled around the house and walked up and down the narrow path, pressing on the kitchen door and examining the gate. He followed the pathway back to the yard, bent low to the ground, and peered for some time at the grass surrounding the stepping stones that made a dotted line from the patio to the gazebo.

"Did you examine the summer house?" he asked, stepping inside the round little building.

"We didn't," the inspector admitted. "I do not see how it would be important. If another intruder were here, Asa Andrews must have seen him, but the young man has not made any such claim."

"Where does Andrews sleep?"

Gregson pointed to the entrance of the food cellar. "He sleeps there. The female servants sleep off the kitchen, and the butler has a small sitting room cordoned off by a curtain in the wine room."

"Cozy," Holmes commented wryly. "Look here." He pointed to one of the sills circling the gazebo. We stepped close and saw that he was looking at the remains of a cigarette.

"Recently smoked," he observed. "Also, and I'm sure you'll agree, inspector, that this is noteworthy, there are two cigarette ends here, and they are of different brands. One is a Churchman's and one is Sobranie …" he trailed off thoughtfully at this.

At last, Gregson seemed compelled to push the discussion onward. "So two people were in the gazebo. Are you sure they must have been here last night?"

Holmes picked up the spent smoke and sniffed it delicately. "I'm fairly certain that these are recently smoked. We know it was not yesterday, as your men would have noticed. Why would Mr. Andrews not mention others in the yard? He can see clearly into the gazebo when he exits the cellar."

"Maybe he came from around the side," I suggested.

"That may be true, but that brings up another question. Where was he coming from? Besides, I see clear evidence in the footprints that someone, a male, exited the gazebo hastily – I can see because he did not bother to stay on the stones – and entered the patio. This could only have been Andrews."

"So our gardener was in the gazebo?" Gregson murmured. "That is not what he told us. He said he had just transplanted a potted plant to the flower bed when he heard the commotion."

Holmes stepped smoothly to the rows of flowers. "There is no pot here and no evidence that any of these plants have recently been transplanted, so we know he is lying about this, at least. But does that mean he is the killer?"

The question seemed to be rhetorical, so Gregson and I stayed quiet as the detective made a few more careful laps around the yard.

A thought struck me. "If there was another occupant in the gazebo, did you track any of their footprints to see how they escaped notice? If they slipped around to the alley, they must have run across the grass."

Holmes worried his lip, staring so intently at the ground that I wondered if he had heard me. I was certain he had, but he seemed strangely disinclined to answer. I got the impression he was perturbed that I had brought the idea up.

"Let's take a look at the study," he said finally, ignoring my query, and we returned to the house. The study was accessible, as Miss Lucille had said, from both the hall and the parlor. We entered through the parlor, and Holmes gave the room a cursory examination, focusing primarily on the carpet, before following its exit to the hall. Exactly opposite was the doorway to the kitchen.

Holmes entered. The room was spacious with ample room for food preparation and a modern range. To the side was a good-sized room, half blocked by curtains, where our maid Lucille and the cook slept.

Holmes went straight to the faded green backdoor and put his face very close to the hasp latch above the doorknob. He made a little hum of excitement and quickly withdrew his little lockpick case which also housed a small assortment of tweezers. He used one of these to carefully remove something from the latch, holding it up to the light for us to see.

Gregson squinted at it, struggling. "Is that part of a string, Mr. Holmes?"

"Indeed. This cast new light on the assumption that no one could have fled from this exit and secure it behind them."

"Curiouser and curiouser," the inspector murmured.

"Clearer and clearer," Holmes corrected. "Are the son and daughter home?"

As Gregson led us upstairs, he wondered, "If we know Andrews came from the gazebo to the study, and there was another person in the gazebo with him, could this mysterious visitor be the murderer who then fled through the study and out of the back entrance? Could Andrews be covering for them?"

Holmes made a non-committal noise in the back of his throat. "This would have to be someone he cares enough about to face the noose alone to shield them. But we do not yet have enough data to know, so there is no use speculating."

Miss Philips, nee Villiers, permitted us into her chambers with polite grace. She was an exceptionally pretty girl with rounded cheeks and large dark eyes. Her face was marked with clear signs of grief. Dark smudges marred the delicate skin around her eyes, and they were red from weeping. Despite this, she held her composure admirably and bid us to sit. Holmes, who had already begun quite impertinently perusing her room, sat last.

Two beautiful Irish Setters lay at her feet, looking melancholy. I wondered how aware they were of their master's death. It seemed to me that we often underestimated animals and their capacity to feel. They whined softly.

"I do not have much to tell you, gentleman," she began as she sat, petting the head of one of the pups absently. "I was up here in my room when I heard Lucille scream. I rushed downstairs to find her at the doorway to my stepfather's parlor. Inside," here her voice broke, "I saw Asa standing next to him. Waterhouse, the butler, was speaking loudly to Asa, asking him what he had done, I think. I can't really remember. I couldn't really focus on anything else but the sight-" she choked off and took a moment to control herself. "Someone fetched the police, and I was led to the sitting room where I remained until they arrived."

"Who led you to the sitting room?" Holmes asked.

Her face scrunched in concentration. "I'm not sure. I think it was Lucille. I apologize. I remember as if through a fog." She took a deep breath. "What will happen to Asa? Surely, he cannot be condemned simply for being in the room?"

Gregson cringed. "That would depend on the jury, miss."

She paled even more. "Oh dear Lord. That cannot be."

"You do not believe he is guilty?" Holmes asked, speaking for the first time. "Even if there seems to be no one else who could have committed this crime?"

She shook her head. "No, sir. I know he did not do it."

"How do you know?"

She struggled for an answer before reasserting feebly, "I just know it, sir."

"When you have eliminated all other possibilities, whatever remains must be the truth."

She leveled a determined and confident look at the detective. "Have you eliminated all else? I know you have not since Asa did not kill my father."

I could tell Holmes was impressed by her demeanor. He gave her one of his all-encompassing quick glances and then stood. "You may very well be right, miss. By the by, did you hear the dogs barking before the tragedy?"

She hesitated, then responded with certainty, "Yes, a little before we heard the clashing and clanging."

"How long a pause was between the barking and the commotion?"

"Oh, about five minutes, sir."

"Do your dogs normally bark?"

"As you can see, no. Only if they feel threatened."

Holmes gazed at her for a long moment, a twinkle of satisfaction in his eyes. Finally, he dipped his chin at her, and we politely excused ourselves.

The son was not much help. With a restless and preoccupied wiggle of his knees, he told us he had gone to the Princess Theater at 8 o'clock by way of the family driver before disembarking a few blocks away and choosing to walk to take in the pleasant evening air. He returned a little past eleven to the police in his home and his father murdered.

The driver in the small carriage house attached to the east side of the home confirmed this tale. He had driven the young man about halfway to the theater, let him out, and then retrieved him from the theater at eleven. They had made haste to return, as the driver had informed the son that something terrible had happened at home.

"Why do people kill, Watson?" Holmes asked as we three were back on the pavement outside the quiet house.

Gregson and I glanced at each other. "As you have often said, money, love, revenge, or self-preservation."

"Correct. I believe narrowing down motive will provide us with the answer."

"Some more recent theories suggest that some may be prone to violence with no motive," Gregson supplied.

Holmes frowned, "While I applaud you keeping abreast of current ideas, and I don't disagree, I believe this is rare. Madmen surely exist, but they are usually easily recognizable and lack the foresight to plan their crimes. Besides, if you are right and this is simply a well-functioning madman who committed this crime for the thrill of it, then I have no power to track him down. A motiveless crime is one of the hardest to investigate."

"So," Gregson continued, taking the rebuff with aplomb, "you believe the killer came through the patio from the alley, killed Philips, and to avoid the gardener coming from the gazebo (doing lord knows what) he slips through the study, across the hall while the maid's back is turned, and exits the backdoor, securing it behind him with-"

"String," Holmes finished. He made a quick pulling motion with his hand, as if mimicking the jerk of the string to force the latch closed. "Child's play, really."

"So Asa Andrews was simply a casualty?"

Holmes looked thoughtful. "I'm reserving judgment on that point, Gregson. Where is the young man being kept?"

"You can see him at the Old Bailey."

"And did Mr. Philips have a personal secretary?"

"Yes, a Mr. Evans. I haven't spoken to him."

He provided us with the address, and we bid him adieu, fetching a cab to visit the secretary near Shepard's Street.

"Where there is a will, there is a way," Holmes quipped as we settled ourselves in the cramped seat. "There's a banality to it, but it often proves true that a will sheds light on why a murder occurs. Philips was a wealthy man; it would be naïve of us to fail to look into how all that wealth is going to be dispersed."

Holmes surprised me by ordering the driver to stop near a carriage depot. He hopped out and disappeared inside for a few moments before returning with an air of satisfaction. He would not tell me what the detour was about, no matter how I pressed him.

"Surely it is all clear to you, Watson," he responded obliquely.

"Not at all," I confessed.

He shrugged and would say no more until we reached Shepard's Street. We were allowed into the small flat by a servant who clearly thought we were official police, and Holmes did nothing to dissuade her of that belief, much to my silent chagrin.

Mr. Evans had evidently heard the news of his employer's death. He held himself with professionalism, but I could tell the death of Mr. Philips had affected him. He told us he had very little time but permitted us to sit down at his small desk in the office off his sitting room.

"I assume you're curious about the status of the family's inheritance? I don't believe in coincidences," he stated matter-of-factly, "so I feel obligated to tell you that there have been some recent alterations to the will."

Holmes lifted a surprised eyebrow. "Has been? Past tense?"

"Just yesterday, in fact."

"That's curious. Usually, one is killed to prevent possible alterations. What was changed?"

"Mr. Philips made most of his money in engines. He sold his business about five years ago to his business partner. He was a good man and wished his estate to be split evenly between his son and step-daughter, with a small amount given to certain charities."

"And now?"

"That all remains. You see, in the original will, he had stipulated – much to the stepdaughter's consternation – that she only be given her portion once she married a man by the name of Mr. Elms. A gentleman old enough to be her father," he ended meaningfully.

"Why ever for?" I exclaimed.

Mr. Evans sighed. Philips was a good man but old-fashioned. He worried that she would not be taken care of if she weren't married well. Mr. Elms was his good friend."

"And, as you said, she was not pleased with this?" Holmes asked.

"Not at all. It was a source of tension between them. She declared that she would not marry anyone she did not wish to, no matter the financial repercussions."

"If she believed that was the state of the will this would mean she would have no motive to kill the old man," I commented.

"Miss Adelaide could not murder anyone," Evans asserted firmly. "For money or any other reason. However, that stipulation is exactly what Mr. Philips removed. He had come to his senses that it was unfair to put such requirements on her, even in an effort to protect her. It was removed yesterday."

"Did she know he was going to remove that condition?"

"I'm not sure. He indicated to me that he had not spoken of it to his children, but one of them may have figured it out in some other way."

"You said you did not believe Adelaide capable of murder, but what of the son?"

Evans leaned back, taking a deep breath. "I don't see him doing something so extreme, but he has some resentment to his father over Adelaide. He insisted she was not really family, so no inheritance should go to her whether she was married or not. Of course, he was aware that Adelaide was refusing her stepfather's arranged betrothal, so he really had nothing to fear on that point."

"Until yesterday."

Evans nodded. "Until yesterday."

"What do you think of the gardener?"

The man across from us frowned in confusion. "I hardly know the boy. Our paths don't have many reasons to cross."

"Did you know he was arrested for the murder?"

"That is surprising. What possible reason could he have to want to see the old man dead?"

Holmes rose. "That's what we are hoping to discover when we speak to him."

Asa Andrews was a fair-haired, handsome young man whose face, while lined with stress, was refreshingly open. He sat on the other side of the old dilapidated table secured in cuffs. He seemed suspicious of us until Holmes introduced himself. He, like Lucille, had been made aware of Holmes's reputation through an apparently healthy line of communication between the neighborhood's servants.

He leaned his head back and closed his eyes in relief. "Oh, thank the heavens. If anyone can prove I'm innocent, it's you."

"A minute," Holmes forestalled, clasping his hands on the table. "Much of what I am able to do for you depends upon you, young man, and how honest you are with us. Tell us what happened the night of the murder. "

"I was in the yard, transplanting some plants from their pots-"

"Were you?" Holmes interrupted.

Perhaps I imagined it, but the boy's face paled. He pushed bravely on though, stubborn in this lie. "Yes, it's best to transplant at night to avoid stressing the plant." He paused, obviously expecting Holmes to contradict him, but the detective remained silent, staring expectantly at him. "I heard the dogs barking near the patio door which was odd because they don't bark often."

"Could you see the patio door?"

"Not where I was sitting. It was blocked by some trees. In any case, it never occurred to me that something terrible was happening, so I continued my work. Then, I heard some commotion, like clattering, as if something had been knocked over."

"How long between the barking and the clattering?"

"About five minutes."

Holmes nodded, clearly pleased that this aligned with the daughter's remembrance.

"At that," the boy continued, "I went to see what was going on. The patio door was ajar, and the dogs were whining as if they were scared to go inside. I called out to Mr. Philips and entered carefully. I saw him sitting at his chair and the table with his teapot and cup lying on its side. I had the thought that he must have dozed off and accidentally hit the thing with his elbow, but I was worried that the sound had not woken him. He is an older man, you know. *Was* an older man," he amended softly. "Someone began knocking on the hall door, but I had touched his shoulder and realized there was blood everywhere, so I didn't answer. I felt too shocked to speak. Before I knew it, Waterhouse was inside yelling at me and Miss Lucille was screaming. After that, it becomes a bit of a blur, but no matter what I told the police, they seemed to believe I had killed him. And they brought me here." He lifted his shackled hands in helplessness.

Holmes considered him for a long while. The boy held fast for an admirable amount of time before he began to shift uncomfortably in his seat.

"What were you really doing in the yard?" he asked the prisoner quietly.

"As I said, I was tending to the flower pots."

"You were not. Don't insult us by continuing to insist on this."

"What does it matter?" the boy asked, clearly frustrated. "I could have been practicing the waltz, and it means nothing of significance to what happened."

"You were not alone."

At this, Mr. Andrew's face went very white. "I'm not sure how you came to that conclusion, sir. I was outside by myself."

"We found two types of cigarettes discarded in the gazebo, where your footsteps emerge."

The boy clutched compulsively at his own fingers. "They must have been there before, sir. I was alone in the garden, as I said."

Holmes leaned back, running a tired hand across his face. "You realize, young man," he began wearily, "that if you were not alone, there is a witness who can corroborate your story and prove that you were in the gazebo at the time your late employer was being murdered? This minor point, as you seem hell-bent on framing it, may make the difference between your freedom and a noose?"

The boy looked down at his lap in defeat. "And you believe there is no way to prove my innocence outside of that?"

"There may not be."

There was a protracted silence. We could hear the muted jingle of the guard's keychain on the other side of the door.

"I was alone," he finally said, his voice so soft that I hardly heard him.

Holmes looked dismayed by this, but he nodded and stood. "So be it. I'll do what I can for you."

"Mr. Andrews," I leaned forward across the desk imploringly, "All you have to do is provide the name of your companion and we can prove your alibi."

He said nothing and I, begrudgingly, rose and followed Holmes through the courthouse to the pleasant air of the descending evening, so at contrast to the grim reality of the silent prisoner inside the bars of the building.

Holmes looked upwards at the pink and orange dusk and let out a long breath.

"I don't understand, Holmes."

"You don't?" he asked in surprise. "You see but you do not observe. The parts are all here. If you could make the connections, it would all be clear to you."

I struggled. It was like peering into the darkness to make the details of a shape visible.

He jerked his head and bid me to walk with him. "I see the chain of events as if I witnessed them myself. The issue is proving it."

"Can you lower yourself to explain it all to me?" I asked with some irritation.

"Of the two children, who had more reason to kill their father?"

"The son," I answered confidently. "He was likely trying to do so before he amended his will but was not aware that he had already done so. But he was at the theater."

"Was he?"

"The driver said-"

"That he had taken him halfway and then let him out."

"You believed he doubled back?"

"It would be easy to do. Perhaps a bit of a walk, but the boy is young. And, in fact, when I stopped by the depot I was able to learn that a man bearing his features rented a cab to the theater a little after nine."

"So he doubled back through the alley, entered the patio – which Andrews could not see from the gazebo – and killed the old man, exiting through the study and the kitchen. Following that, he rushed to the carriage depot and paid for a ride to the theater."

"He attempted to create an alibi – more than our man Andrews has done – but no alibi is perfect unless it is authentic."

"But why would the dogs bark at him? And why did there seem to be a struggle when Philips was evidently killed in his chair?"

"As to the dogs, they are excellent judges of character, so that's a point that is possibly testable. The façade of a struggle is vitally important and illuminates the heart of this case."

He fell silent, and I understood that he was hoping I could draw the same conclusions he had. I ruminated on it until I came to the only answer I could think of.

"Staging a struggle, a loud one, would ensure that the body was found. He wanted to draw attention to it. But why? Why would he run that risk when he could have slipped out without notice?"

"What end did it accomplish?" Holmes asked simply.

"It led to Asa's arrest. You mean to say, that he was meant to be framed for this?"

"I believe so. Further," we were approaching Scotland Yard, "I believe that both occupants of the gazebo were meant to be framed, but the mystery guest instead slipped around to the front of the house."

Realization dawned on me. "And seemed, from Lucille's perspective, to be coming down the stairs from her room," I finished. "So it was Adelaide in the gazebo with Andrews. Whatever were they doing?" I wondered.

Holmes made a full stop and turned to stare at me with an expression equal mix of disbelief and amusement.

"Oh," I realized, flushing a bit, "Of course."

"I thought that would be immediate to you. After all, you are three-continent Watson," he remarked with an aggravating smirk.

"That was a jest, Holmes," I growled.

"Mmmm, in any case, you can understand why the young man seems adamant to keep her presence out of it."

"How do we prove this?"

"That is what I'm working on," he tapped his head.

"The string," I pointed out.

"What of it?"

"He doesn't know you removed it."

Holmes frowned and then he beamed with pride. "Good man! That is brilliant! The servant's area in the kitchen would be sufficient…" he murmured thoughtfully. "Let's gather our friend, Gregson, for the denouement."

We arrived back at the Philips' house when it was well after nightfall. Waterhouse answered and was more than amenable to our little plan.

Holmes and I were waiting comfortably in the sitting room when Adelaide and Grant came in to see us. Holmes stood and shook the son's hand.

"Forgive our intrusion at this difficult time. Inspector Gregson has removed his men and considers this a resolved case, but I have my reservations. May we have your permission to continue our investigation? I'm particularly interested in your kitchen and that hasp lock. I have some theories as to how it was secured from the outside, and I am hoping that there may be some evidence remaining."

"I have no objection," Adelaide said.

At the same time, her stepbrother frowned. "Whatever for? It seems you're grasping at straws, sir. I can't fathom why you are going so far as to protect that little traitor."

Adelaide looked supremely uncomfortable while I tried desperately to appear as if I did not notice.

"It has nothing to do with protection," Holmes answered brusquely. "There are inexcusable unanswered questions in relation to this murder that seriously cast doubt on Mr. Andrews' guilt. I cannot believe you would tolerate an innocent man going to gaol for something he did not do."

"He was the only one there. He was standing over the body mere seconds after the murder occurred. I don't see what is unanswered."

Holmes nodded and stood. "Very well then."

Adelaide rose quickly, her face flush with panic. "Sir!"

Holmes waved her off. "There is nothing I can do without permission to examine the house."

"I give you permission!" she declared.

"You speak out of turn, Adelaide," her stepbrother barked. "This isn't your house."

She looked at Holmes with a desperation that was difficult to endure, and even more difficult to ignore as we must. Holmes shook his head in defeat and moved from the room as the two siblings began arguing behind us.

On the front porch, Waterhouse was waiting with the two Irish Setters. He passed them to us dutifully, and I held their leashes as we circled to the tree-covered dirt alleyway that led to the gate and kitchen door. The gate opened with a low creak, and we stood at the kitchen door for a moment, waiting.

The silence stretched on and I began to feel my heart sink. Perhaps we had misjudged what he would do-

Something banged against the door. We could hear the sounds of a brief struggle and Gregson's recognizable voice ordering someone to sit.

The latch made no sound as it was drawn back, and the green door swung open silently to the kitchen. Grant Philips was sitting at the table, Gregson's cuffs secured around his wrists. The door to the hall opened at the same time that I stepped in with the dogs who began to bark in earnest at the young man.

He hisses and shoved at them with his foot. "Get those mangy dogs away from me," he spat.

"See?" said Holmes. "What did I say, Watson? Excellent judges of character."

I managed to get them outside, wrapping their leashes around one of the gate's bars.

When I stepped back into the kitchen, Adelaide stood at the other door, framed by the gaslight flooding the hall, her mouth open in shock. "What is happening, sirs?" she demanded.

"I caught your brother red-handed removing key evidence," Gregson accused.

"What exactly did you see?" Holmes pressed.

"He came in here and dug out the string you had Waterhouse wrap around the hasp latch and put it into his pocket."

At this revelation, young Mr. Philips paled and slumped in his chair.

"Capital!" Holmes declared. "I trust this, along with the information from the carriage depot, will be enough to get dear Andrews out of gaol?"

"I'll drag the dogs up for testimony if I have to, Holmes," Gregson declared.

"Someone tell me exactly what is going on!" Adelaide insisted.

"Your brother here savagely murdered your father because he knew he

was intending to change his will to allow you equal inheritance with no stipulations regarded your marital arrangements," Holmes explained. "A change that was made yesterday, unbeknownst to Grant."

At this news, the scoundrel chuckled darkly under his breath and closed his eyes in resignation.

"He intended to implicate not only Asa, but Asa's mystery guest as well, but that did not quite go as planned."

Holmes did not specify, but he gave Adelaide a meaningful look that spoke volumes. Her face turned red, and she dashed from the room in distress.

"It doesn't matter," Grant commented idly. "I can still ruin her when I confess to the whole thing at the trial."

"And then you'll hang," Holmes snapped.

Gregson pulled him up roughly. "Quite a mouth you have on you, for someone whose days are numbered. Come along."

He was bustled out of the house roughly onto the street where more of Gregson's men were now waiting, but we did not follow. We ascended the stairs, and Holmes knocked softly on the open door to Adelaide's chamber.

We entered without being bid to. The young lady was standing at the window, looking out into the distance. When she turned, she pressed a hand to her stomach and wiped wayward strands of hair from her face, clearly attempting to gather herself.

"I'm sorry," she said with a wavering voice, "I should not have behaved in such a manner. I simply cannot believe Grant would do such a thing for money. It's only money."

Holmes cleared his throat. "We do not believe it was simply for money."

Her eyes filled with tears. "I see." She vacillated and then asked, "How did you know? That I was in the summer house with Asa?"

"The particular citric scent of one of the cigarettes left there was present in your room. Distinctly feminine footprints were clearly visible in the grass fleeing towards the alley and turning back towards the front of the house," Holmes explained gently. "For what it may be worth, Mr. Andrews said nothing of his relationship with you. I believe he would have gone to his execution protecting you. He clearly loves you very much."

She swiped at the moisture on her cheeks. "I would not have allowed him to. I was hoping you could save him before I had to say anything."

"You needn't say anything now. It isn't necessary. And anything your darling brother feels compelled to announce will be quickly disregarded as the anger of a bitter man."

"You are a wealthy woman, Miss Adelaide," I said softly, "and while it may be unorthodox, I imagine this will allow you freedom to choose a husband you desire."

"I lose one man I care deeply for and gain another," she observed. "My feelings are understandably conflicted."

Holmes nodded, and we left her there to come to terms with them in her own time.

'My collection of M's is a fine one. Moriarty himself is enough to make any letter illustrious, and here is Morgan the poisoner, and Merridew of abominable memory, and Mathews, who knocked out my left canine in the waiting-room at Charing Cross-' The Adventure of the Empty House

After the dark, blood-soaked winter of 1888 had passed, lightened only by the happy start of my blissful matrimony to my dear Mary, Mrs. Hudson once remarked to me on one of my sporadic visits to Baker Street that Holmes's routine had become strangely quiet. He was abed before eleven at night and up before eight in the morning. It was not a condition of his boarding agreement, but on those days of inactivity, he often descended to the kitchen and spoke to our doting landlady while helping her here and there as she put together one of her hearty and serviceable breakfasts. I knew that Holmes, with my constant urging, had made a valiant effort to put away those appalling tendencies I so lamented when we resided together. We never spoke of it at length, but after he was free from the inevitably crushing weight of that dreaded morphine and cocaine concoction that had threatened to derail his illustrious career (and, frighteningly, his mind) in those dark years after 1888, it seemed he was aware that he needed to stay busy in whatever capacity he could, no matter how trivial, lest he slip back into harmful habits.

It was thus very surprising to feel his large hand shaking me awake a little after two in the morning on a chill Wednesday in the early spring of 1891. My wife had left for an extended stay in the country with Mrs. Forrester to see her previous charge through a mild illness, so I was once again taking up bed in the room of my bachelor days. I admit to feeling an initial surge of irritation at the sight of his shadow looming over me considering I had a long day of patient visits ahead of me and needed to be well rested and ready in only five hours.

Holmes, ever prescient, sensed my annoyance. "Very sorry to knock you up so early, old man. Lestrade felt this was an appropriate time to pay us a visit."

I blinked up at him blearily. "Is it regarding a case?"

"I cannot imagine he'd come to us at this ungodly hour if he did not deem the matter to be of some urgency. You aren't obliged to sit in, of course, but I thought it best to give you that choice."

The blissful warmth of the soft mattress pulled me down, but I fought off my bed covers and shook my head, too tempted by the possibility of adventure.

Holmes left me to get dressed, and I shucked on some trousers and wrapped myself in my own worn out dressing gown.

Lestrade was seated in the wicker seat, drinking from his small hip flask.

Holmes stretched his bare feet towards the newly lit fire in the grate as I took my customary chair across from him.

"My apologies," Lestrade started, looking rumpled but wide awake. "Your landlady was not quite pleased to see me."

"That was readily deduced by how loudly she pounded on my bedroom door," Holmes responded ruefully.

Lestrade looked embarrassed. "Yes, yes. She made a hardy effort to be polite to me, so I worried she might redirect her anger towards you. I trust you have experience smoothing her ruffled feathers."

"You didn't come here from Scotland Yard," Holmes observed abruptly, as was his wont. "You came to us from your home."

Lestrade took the observation in stride, nodding. "True, though I had been at Scotland Yard late into the night." He fell silent, looking pensive.

Holmes cast me an amused but tired look after a protracted silence. "Not to rush you, inspector, but the dear doctor here must decide if he needs to ask Agar to take on his patients."

Lestrade cleared his throat. "Did you read about the accident near St. James Square yesterday?"

Holmes frowned. "No, there was nothing in the papers today."

Lestrade hummed. "Might show up on the morning edition, if even then. On the face of it, the whole thing is a simple tragic accident, hardly worth reporting on, I'm sure. Around nine in the evening, Mrs. Mathews stepped in front of a four-wheeler and was trampled to death." He cringed and then continued, "An unpleasant way to exit this world."

"Unpleasant and tragic, but I fail to see the mystery."

"Well, some in her social circle say that her behavior has been erratic the past few weeks."

Holmes cocked his head curiously. "Erratic in what way?"

"Speaking to herself, or rather, speaking as if to voices only she could hear. Paranoia and apparent hallucinatory incidents."

"Hallucinations and paranoia?" I interjected. "Those symptoms often indicate mental deterioration of the sort that could explain the action, whether accidental or purposeful, that led to her death."

"Indeed, indeed," Lestrade murmured, falling into pensive silence once again, pulling absently at the ends of his neglected mustache.

"Inspector," Holmes urged with startling gentleness considering his usual nature and the unpleasantly early hour, "Who precisely is in this 'social circle', as you call it?"

"Mrs. Mathews' stepdaughter spoke to me." He hesitated. "As did my wife."

"Ah, I see. And how does your lovely wife know the late Mrs. Mathews?"

"They are friends from the Somerville Club. They met almost a year ago and got on immediately."

"And are you here seeking my help at your wife's behest?"

Lestrade, apparently sensing some censure in the detective's tone, flushed up defensively. "I'm here, and this may be difficult for you to understand, because I have come to trust my wife's instincts. And, yes, scoff all you wish, but her concern is my concern, and I wish to address it for her peace of mind."

Holmes stared impassively at him for a long while before speaking, his voice flat and carefully measured, "I did not scoff, Lestrade." He looked into the roaring fire, his expression lit by the orange flames and the angles of his face sharply shadowed. He seemed deep in thought.

"Tell me about the Mathews' household," he said at last.

"Mr. Mathews is from a decidedly middle-class family from Horley. He's now some hoity-toity textile importer specializing in materials from China, since that's all the rage right now. He has a daughter, about thirteen, from his first marriage. The first wife died fairly soon after the birth of the child, I believe. He married Mrs. Mathews seven years ago, and they live in a nice bijou flat on King Street now."

"In wedded bliss?"

"As far as I know, but I'm more familiar with the lady than the couple."

"Have you spoken to Mr. Mathews since her death? Does he seem affected?"

"Gregson handled the case. He said Mathews seems affected, though he has admirable control over himself."

This time, Holmes did scoff. "Of course, I forget that it is difficult to gauge the depths of a gentleman's grief seeing as he is expected to conceal it. Did the child have a good relationship with her stepmother? Did she seem affected?"

"She was a right mess, clearly in shock."

Holmes straightened, clapping his hands with resolved finality. "Very well then. I'm not sure what can be mined from this incident, but if it is sufficient enough to worry your better half, then it is sufficient enough for me to take a look. After all, if you cannot call on your friends for favors, who can you rely on?"

Lestrade flushed in surprise at being elevated to so high a status and stood quickly, coughing to cover the moment. "Many thanks, Holmes. Would you like to see the site of the accident?"

"Was this accident witnessed?"

"Yes, by approximately twenty people."

"Then, no. I don't think that's a priority. I likely do not need to prove she walked in front of the horses, but I do need to deduce why. I assume she has not been buried?"

"No, she's still at the morgue."

"We'll start there. We-" he gave me a questioning glance which I answered with a quick nod "-will visit the morgue at ten. Perhaps the good doctor and I can get in a bit of sleep."

"That should do nicely," Lestrade agreed, "the funeral will not be for a few days. Thank you again, Holmes. I did not know the lady beyond the few friendly visits she bestowed on my wife, but she seemed a nice, gentle-hearted sort, and if there is any trickery here, I'd like to get to the bottom of it."

Holmes steadfastly ignored my suppressed yawns on the way to the Westminster coroner. I do not believe he went back to sleep after Lestrade left Baker Street, but he somehow looked impeccable in his smart morning coat and expensive embroidered waistcoat. I brushed self-consciously at the slight wrinkles in my hastily knotted cravat, but my friend did not seem to notice, lost deep in thought as he stared out of the carriage window at the passing bustle of the London streets.

The recently built three-story brick building smelled of rotting flesh and the strange pickle-like odour of formaldehyde. Mrs. Mathews' body was behind a curtain on the second story. If I had forgotten the manner of her death, I was cruelly reminded of it when the sheet was pulled back to reveal her face and upper body. Even Holmes took a pause to gather himself before moving forward to examine the body in that minute but efficient way of his that was still so comforting after all these years.

From what I could tell from her bruised and disfigured face, she had been a wispy, delicate blonde. Her collarbones were starkly defined in a way that spoke of recent loss of weight. I noticed a strange look to the pinna of her ear and moved closer in my curiosity.

"Holmes," I said, "she has necrosis here."

The detective stepped next to me with his magnifying glass, his shoulder brushing mine. He hummed under his breath as he analyzed the blackish dead tissue dotting her ear. He scurried down the slab to gently raise her hands to peer at her fingertips and then raised the sheet from her feet and did the same to her toes.

"Did you conduct a full postmortem?" he asked the coroner, a doctor Braxely, as he worked his way systematically up her leg with his face bent close to her skin.

Braxely, a seasoned medical man, gave me a disbelieving look and gestured towards the woman's crushed body. Holmes missed the expression and looked up expectantly.

"I did a cursory examination, of course," the man answered patiently. "The actual cause of her death was injury to her head. Her lung was also collapsed, but she passed before that injury could kill her. Her death was blessedly quick and hopefully painless."

"But you did not examine her organs for any external toxins or for any diseases?"

"I did not think it likely that she expired due to poison at the exact time her head was being crushed by a horse's hoof," the man riposted with irritation.

Holmes let out a quiet, oddly pacifying chuckle and raised the corpse's hand up from the slab once more. "You notice the peculiar gangrene of her fingers and toes?"

Braxely frowned. "I did, and I noted it in my report but, clearly, it is not related to her death."

"Not directly," Holmes murmured. "And, as the observant Dr. Watson pointed out, the necrosis affecting both her ears? Did you make note of that as well?"

"Young man, I make note of every detail I see during my postmortems. Is there a point to this? You clearly suspect some correlation between these details and her existence here on my autopsy table."

"I do." Instead of elaborating, my dear friend gave me an expectant look which caught me by surprise. I floundered, wracking my brain for whatever response he was looking for. I settled on a vague but safe speculation.

"I imagine you believe that Mrs. Mathews was exposed to some sort of toxin." As the words left my mouth, the gears of the much slower and less precise machinery of my own mind began to turn. "And you believe this toxin is responsible for her erratic and ultimately tragic behavior."

Holmes fairly beamed. "Spot on, Watson. The process by which your brain arrived at that conclusion may have been painfully plodding, but you arrived nonetheless to an extremely obvious deduction. Now, what toxin causes hallucinations, paranoia, gangrene, and possibly necrosis of some extremities?"

Braxely and I stared once again at each other. I was admittedly not an expert on rare poisons or natural toxins as Holmes was; much of that esoteric knowledge was merely peripheral to my main general medical practice. From my acquaintance with Holmes, I was familiar with the more common poisoning agents such as arsenic and ricin, but these did not have mental effects. Certain mushrooms, I knew, could cause some vivid hallucinations. I was on the cusp of venturing forth that hesitant guess when Braxely saved me.

"Ergot poisoning," he asserted. "Of course."

"Ergot poisoning?" I echoed. "The fungus that can decimate livestock if they consume affected barley and wheat?"

"Precisely," Holmes confirmed. "The fungus Claviceps purpurea which can grow on many food crops and often eaten by unfortunate animals can cause, among other things, visual and auditory hallucinations, paranoia and disturbed behavior, as well as gangrene of the fingers and toes. Necrosis of pigs' ears has also often been seen in affected animals."

"How would she have been exposed to ergot poisoning?"

Holmes shrugged. "It can grow on bread, particularly rye. She may not have known what it looks like. You know, there are some who speculate that the witch trials of Salem and Norway were caused by consuming ergot-infested bread. The women affected suffered convulsions and unsettling behavior that was interpreted by the highly superstitious and religious communities as being bewitched."

"All those brutal executions, and they may have simply been infected? How horrible," I sympathized.

"One man was pressed to death over the period of three days."

"I'm not sure I'd like to know the details of that."

Holmes smirked. "Fascinating process, actually. But inarguably gruesome - but, hullo, here is Lestrade! Good-morning, Lestrade!"

The official inspector stepped around the curtain, hat in hand and attired in a somber black suit. He gave the body on the table a long, sad look before collecting himself.

"I told my wife that she did not suffer, but it is hard to imagine that is the truth when one looks on damage such as this," he murmured almost as if to himself. He looked up at Holmes. "What's up, then? You look strangely satisfied for one standing in a morgue."

"I believe I have discovered some important details," Holmes announced with some relish.

"Do you care to share them with us mortals?" Lestrade snarled impatiently. He clearly had suffered a fitful few hours of sleep after departing Baker Street.

Holmes graced him with a patently patient look. "I'm endeavoring to help you, Lestrade," he reminded with gentle firmness. "You and your dear wife are evidently very distressed, so I won't bandy the usual barbs with you. But I urge you to remember that, in this case, I am on your side."

The inspector flushed with embarrassment and only nodded brusquely.

"As I was saying," Holmes continued, "Watson and I found some curious details while examining the late Mrs. Mathews' body. You'll notice the ears, as well as the fingers and toes."

Lestrade took a closer look. "Why, they're all black," he said, grimly.

"Dead tissue," Holmes replied in his languid fashion, but I could sense the undercurrent of excitement he was attempting to keep under rein.

The official looked at them with a puzzled expression. "I am no medical man, but an accident such as this would not cause that." He glanced towards me. "Poison?"

I nodded. "It seems very likely."

"So she was drugged, panicked, and that's why she walked in front of the horses?"

Holmes frowned. "Not quite as simple as that. She may have been hallucinating, but we cannot be sure exactly why the accident happened. Furthermore, and more importantly, we cannot be sure how she ingested the poison to begin with."

"Well, clearly, someone fed it to her!" Lestrade exclaimed.

"This particular poison," I interjected, "could possibly be ingested accidentally. Perhaps in bread or some grains."

Lestrade ran an exasperated and tired hand across his face. "So we've circled back around to merely an accident."

Holmes shook his head. "As I said, we cannot be sure. It might be educational to meet the family. Do you believe they would be willing to speak with me?"

In my association with Holmes, I had often followed him into the dark underside of London. This experience had noticeably changed my perspective of the fine, expensive flats of Mayfair, St. James, and the like. The beautiful white-washed villa, the front built right to the kerb with a lovely little garden in the back, struck me with a strange deflated sense of sadness when I thought of all the dim, grimy little hovels populated with hordes of unfortunates in Whitechapel.

On closer inspection, however, I noticed signs of neglect as we stepped from the pavement up the small porch steps and rang the bell. The parts of the garden I could see were marred by a few freshly grown weeds, and the tall windows looking into the sitting room had a thin layer of dust that any respected butler or housekeeper would find unacceptable.

Servant issues became even more evident as the door was opened, not by a doorman, but by a young girl wearing a clean, smart black dress and collar. Her eyes were red from weeping. I guessed this to be the deceased's stepdaughter.

Lestrade removed his hat hastily. "Maddie! I'm not sure if you will remember me, but your mother brought you to our home once-"

"Of course I remember you, Mr. Lestrade," she answered. Her voice was small and tremulous, but her manner was strangely confident for one so young. "Mama brought me to visit your wife a long time ago when I was still at the girl's school. She gave us lemon scones with clotted cream."

Lestrade forced a light chuckle. "Yes, my wife's scones are certainly memorable."

"Are you here because of what happened to mama?"

Lestrade pressed her shoulder comfortingly. "Yes, this is my colleague Sherlock Holmes and his friend, Dr. Watson."

"Oh, mama was so fond of following you in the papers," she told Holmes with wistful sadness. "She always boasted that she shared a mutual friend with the famous detective. I do think she was hoping to meet you."

Holmes blushed, as he was wont to do when unexpectedly praised. "I see. I admit I regret that meeting never happened."

"That's quite all right. I'm sure she would be just tickled to know you were here looking into her death." That same sad wistfulness marred her face. "You may enter, sirs, if you'd like." She stepped aside, and we shuffled into the wide hall.

"Maddie, why are you answering the door to guests? Where is your doorman?"

"Oh, papa let all the servants go."

Lestrade started with surprise and hung up his hat. "All of them? Why ever for?"

"He said he did not trust them not to gossip about mama's … moments of distress."

"How long ago?"

"Approximately three weeks."

"You've been without servants for that long?"

She waved her hand airily. "I know how to cook and make tea and papa made sure everything in the house was in order." She brought us into a large sitting room and bid us sit as she bustled to make tea despite our protestations.

She returned a few moments later with some fragrant tea and a small assortment of finger sandwiches. Holmes forwent the food but sipped on the tea dutifully. I, on the other hand, never passed up some fortifying nourishment and chomped appreciatively on the cucumber sandwiches.

"This is very good tea," Holmes complimented.

"Papa makes his own blends. He says the Chinese know tea even better than we do."

"So I've heard," Holmes agreed. "May I ask you some questions about the days before your mother's death?"

She folded her hands primly across her lap. "I've already told the other inspectors everything, but I'll answer any of your questions, sir."

"Were you close to your stepmother?"

Grief suffused her innocent features. "Yes, we were very close. I do not remember my own mother. She died when I was a baby. Mama – my stepmother – took care of me and loved me as her own."

Holmes gave her a gentle smile. "She sounds lovely. Inspector Lestrade here tells me that you spoke about some strange behavior of hers recently."

She pressed a fretful hand to her forehead and stood, pacing behind the settee as she spoke. "Oh, it's terrible to remember, but she would sometimes talk to herself, even argue with herself."

"With herself or possibly with voices she was hearing?"

"Is there a difference?"

"A minute one, but yes."

"It seemed she was talking to someone else. Once or twice, she was convinced there was a monster in the house. She kept saying 'don't you see it, Maddie?' and trying to hide. It was horrible to watch because she was normally so sensible. She was often dizzy, as well, and complained about her muscles aching."

"Did she ever faint or convulse?"

"Once, during tea, she began to shake violently. I also thought that maybe I was to be a sister soon because she was often sick in her stomach." She flushed a bit. "If you understand …"

"It's all right," Lestrade reassured. "You're doing very well and being very helpful. Now, think carefully. Did anything else strange happen?"

"Well, one time right before bedtime, I caught her trying to leave the house in her dressing gown. It was odd because she seemed distressed, as if she did not want to leave but could not stop herself. I pleaded with her and finally told her she simply could not go outside dressed as she was," she made a firm chopping motion with her hand looking so much older than her tender years, "and she immediately listened to me. Like I was the mother. It was strange and upsetting."

Holmes gave me an intent look. "Extreme compliance? That doesn't fit the pathology of ergot, as far as I know."

"Ergot?" the young girl queried.

"It is a toxin," I explained.

Holmes nodded in confirmation. "We suspect your mother may have been ingesting it, perhaps in something she was eating or drinking accidentally. You say your father blends his own teas? May we look at them?"

All colour drained from the girl's face. "Do you mean to say we may have been inadvertently poisoning her this whole time?"

"That is not exactly what we mean, but I would like to take a peek to be sure," Holmes assured her, already standing.

Following behind her, I could see one of the small pearl buttons that clasped the high neck of her collar was undone, likely overlooked as she had attempted to dress herself without the aid of a lady's-maid. There was no appropriate way to inform her. I saw Holmes's own look catch on the detail, but he had enough common sense to leave it be as well. Such a small thing made me feel a surge of sympathy for the girl now all alone with her father and no female presence to guide and support her.

"Do you have any other family?" I asked.

"My grandmother, my father's mother, is still alive. She lives where my papa used to live out in the country, and he sends her money. My stepmother has a sister who lives in Bristol whom I love very much. She has asked me to come stay with her for a short while, but I can't think of leaving my father while he is grieving."

She brought us into the large kitchen and opened a cupboard, removing an ornate floral tea caddy. Inside, were five matching tea containers tightly capped.

Holmes pulled them free without asking, opening each and sniffing them carefully. He went so far as to shake a few leaves free from each, poking and separating them with his finger and examining them with his lens. Young Maddie watched patiently, a curious but worried expression on her face.

"There is no ergot here," Holmes declared at last. "Only a very interesting mix of Assam and fruit leaves. Also green tea – it seems your father is highly influenced by the east." He smiled at the girl and brushed the leaves into the bin.

Maddie looked understandably relieved to hear this.

"Did your mother have a favorite café or bakery? Some establishment she frequented often?"

"No, sir. We often ate at home. She would occasionally go to the A.B.C. tea shop by her club, but that was not often. I went a few times with her, both to the shop and the club. I had a lovely time with all those bright women!"

A key turning in the latch of the front entryway brought us up short. Holmes quickly rearranged the tea caddy and returned it to its spot. He pressed a finger to his lip conspiratorially.

"Now, Maddie, let's keep this little tour between us for now. No need to upset your father any more than he already is."

By the time we retook the sitting room, her father was opening the door from the hall and entering. He looked startled to see three strange men in his home, naturally.

Holmes broke the ice by striding forward with that casual charm he could adopt like a second skin.

"Mr. Mathews, I presume? My name is Sherlock Holmes. This is my dear friend, Dr. Watson, and Inspector Lestrade of Scotland Yard. Your lovely daughter here was just about to tell us when we could expect you home."

Even though my friend's manner managed to put him a bit at ease, Mr. Mathews still clasped his outstretched hand with guarded weariness. "Is that so? You're the private detective?"

"Consulting detective," Holmes corrected smoothly. "Your wife was acquainted with Lestrade's wife. We're merely here in assurance to her."

"I see," our host responded carefully. He was a man of middle age and wore a face that, from certain angles, made one wonder what any woman could see in him, and from other angles, could pass by without attracting any special notice. His dark hair was thinning, and I could see he was contemplating an ill-advised comb-over to disguise it. His clothes were expensive, though a few years out of trend, and his waistcoat cut from fine, Chinese floral silk.

"Inspector Lestrade, you say?" he continued. "I dealt with your colleagues about this … accident. Gregson, I believe his name was."

"And we mean to cast no aspersion on Gregson, believe you me," Lestrade said clumsily, "He is, in fact, a superior detective. But he did mention in his report that your wife had been demonstrating some odd symptoms in the last few weeks."

"Of course she was. She obviously suffered from a mental break. She killed herself, after all, gentlemen," Mathews responded testily.

I gently touched Maddie's arm and suggested she leave us alone. While I did not want to think too harshly of a man who had recently suffered such a great loss, such a blunt statement should not be uttered in the presence of a young lady. Maddie's face had gone white, but she nodded with admirable equanimity and left the room.

"Forgive me, sir," Holmes began quietly, "but the symptoms described do not align with one in a suicidal state of mind."

"What does it matter? One could hardly stage horses stomping her to death or the twenty or so witnesses who saw it when it happened." The man's voice was angry, and I felt this interview was not going to be productive.

"Who said anything about staging her death?" Holmes asked sharply, his gaze like a hawk.

"No one did, sir, but you are clearly implying that the events were not so cut and dry. And if they are not cut and dry, then they are complicated. I won't have you filling my daughter's head that her mother's death was anything but a tragic accident. Nelda was unwell, and I curse myself that I did not get her help in time. Now, I'm a very busy man, so if you don't mind?"

A few moments later, we found ourselves on the small porch, the black mourning wreath rattling against the closed door.

"Hum," Holmes grunted under his breath and took off down the street without a word. Lestrade and I followed quickly.

"Well, Holmes, what are you thinking?" Lestrade demanded.

"He is responsible for his wife's death," Holmes responded simply. "It was no tragic accident but a premeditated murder. And I will find out how he did it, mark my words."

"I can't say I disagree, but what makes you so certain, Holmes?" Lestrade demanded.

"Her symptoms indicate that she was poisoned consistently over a period of time. It's only logical to conclude that it was someone in consistent close contact with her. Her only company the past few weeks had been her stepdaughter and her husband. Now, I highly doubt young Maddie is capable of such a dastardly deed."

"There seems to be no motive," Lestrade mused. "He is obviously doing well financially, if the material of his suit is any indication."

"Eh? I didn't realize you had an eye for high-end fashion, Lestrade," Holmes riposted good-naturedly.

"Well, clearly not as much an eye as you do, Holmes." It was meant as a slight, but the barb had the opposite effect on Holmes, who pressed an exaggerated hand to his chest and smiled.

"My dear Lestrade! I had no idea you held my attire in such high regard."

Flustered, Lestrade struggled to regain control of the interaction. "Stop fishing for compliments, Mr. Holmes."

"I have to fish," Holmes waved off airily as he continued down the street. "Watson is frugal with his praise, always scolding me about this or that."

"I can't imagine why."

"Ha! In any case, my suits benefit greatly from a well-skilled tailor. I did some work for a prominent figure, who shall remain unnamed, and of the many gifts I received for my services was free access to their tailor. I have their card here. Tell them Sherlock Holmes sent you and you'll likely get a free fitting." Holmes pulled out a card and held it between two fingers.

Lestrade took it, red-faced. "Huntsman?" he exclaimed. He cocked a curious eyebrow at my friend. "A prominent figure, hmm? I suppose I know better than to ask."

Holmes tapped his nose conspiratorially. "One lesser known perk to my chosen career, inspector."

After lunch, Holmes emerged from his room and, after gulping down a cup of coffee, departed without a word.

I put my notes on the three beryls case in some sort of rudimentary order and then settled down to catch up on the newspapers before dinner.

Holmes returned a moment before the clock struck four o'clock.

"Try to guess what I discovered, Watson!" he exclaimed, barging into the room and startling me into an unmanly gasp of surprise.

I straightened my copy of the *Times* with a huff. "That the earth revolves around the sun?"

He drew up short, giving me a wickedly amused glare. "We'll pin that debate for a later time, old man. No, I discovered that our dear Mr. Mathews is in dire financial straits." He plopped himself on his favourite armchair and propped his feet up on the raggedy footstool. "I made a quick visit to his import warehouse and it was," he made a cutting motion across his neck, "dead. Empty. There is no importing going on there. It appears to have been derelict for at least a year."

"But his clothing is very expensive," I protested.

"And who knows how much coin he spends to keep up that façade. You may not have the 'eye' that I am accused of having, but surely you noticed that his waistcoat had been mended more than once and was a season out of style. Of course, to a casual observer, those small details are easy to overlook. I doubt many people know the reality of the state of his business. And I unearthed more salient details. Someone – I'll give you one guess as to who - recently took out a life insurance policy on Mrs. Mathews from the Bank of England. For 1000 pounds."

"So we have motive."

"And I think I have a clear idea of the means, though it may require a trip to Horley, if you're up to it."

"Horley? Mathews' childhood home?"

"I began to wonder when I saw the empty warehouse – where does Mathews go every day if he isn't going to his job? He could be spending time at a club or engaging in some pleasurable activity, but I also checked with the Charing Cross train station and discovered that a person of Mathews' description regularly purchases a ticket to Horley"

"How regularly?"

"At least three times a week for the past two months. One ticket seller took particular notice of the *Chinoiserie* style of his clothing."

"How does this help you if you think he poisoned his wife with the tea?"

"I need to get my hands on that tea to prove my hypothesis. Perhaps he has stored it somewhere safe when not in use. Check the copy of Bradshaw and see when the earliest train is, please."

We were in Horley as the sun began to dip close to the horizon, spilling pinkish hues across the sky. The older Mrs. Mathews lived in a little two-story brick house that seemed to embody his modest upbringing. There was an enclosed garden in the back that gave way, through a small waist-high stone wall, to an expansive field of wildflowers. Holmes stared at it for a long moment before nodding to himself and opening the small little gate to enter the front yard.

An older woman, clearly the housekeeper, answered with a gruff greeting, her voice marred as if she had spent her whole life drinking hard spirits.

"Good evening," said Holmes jovially, "My name is Peterson and this is my associate Mills. We're horticulturalists visiting your town to view the spring wildflowers. We noticed your beautiful yard and wondered if we could take a closer look. Is your master or mistress at home?"

"Eh?" the woman barked as if hard of hearing. "The flowers?"

"Yes, ma'am."

"Come in then. I'll get the mistress and see if she wants to bother coming down to speak to you."

Holmes smiled brightly. "Many thanks."

We were shown into a small drawing room dotted with plants and an old sheepdog that only lifted its heavy head at us before rolling over and going back to sleep.

The minute the door was closed behind us, Holmes was up and pressing his ear to it. Apparently satisfied that our wizened hostess was out of the hall, he opened the door and gestured for me to follow him.

I was fairly certain that the only ones in the house were Mr. Mathews' mother and the elderly housekeeper, so I felt no mortal fear at being caught sneaking around, but as a gentleman, I still felt a spike of panic at the idea of being detained by the local constabulary who, I'm sure, would not look too kindly on two men skulking about a widow's home uninvited.

Holmes headed straight for the kitchen, and we swung through the green baize door into a small, serviceable kitchen. Holmes immediately began opening and closing cabinets, and I followed suit, desperate to be back in the drawing-room before we were caught in this embarrassingly inappropriate behavior.

"Holmes!" I whispered urgently, kneeling down to the cabinet near the sink. "Look at this." I pulled out a small tea container that was the exact same floral design as the one we'd seen in Mr. Mathews' kitchen.

"Hullo!" Holmes said excitedly, snatching it from me. He made to open it when his movements were arrested by a shuffling in the room above us and a creak of an unstable step. He shoved the tea into a pocket of his morning coat and rushed me out of the room.

By the time the drawing room doors were opened to let in the mistress of the house, Holmes and I were posed respectably in our chairs.

Mrs. Mathews and her housekeeper made an apt pair, both a bit haggard and distrustfully puzzled by our appearance in their quiet home.

Holmes introduced himself under our assumed names once more, ever the gentleman even in the face of the lady's irritation and disbelief.

"We don't get many visitors up here," she squinted at us, "you're horologists, you say?"

"Horticulturalists. We merely request permission to walk about your garden and beyond to look at the flowers."

"Bit odd, isn't it? Never heard of men eager to frolic in flowers," she snorted in the most unladylike way.

Holmes laughed in that light manner that was efficient at putting people at ease. "It's our specialization, ma'am."

"Well, if you want to traipse around the foliage, go right ahead. Just mind the rose bushes near the back door because they're delicate, and I don't want you ruining my hard work."

"Of course, madam." Holmes tipped his chin, and we were shown around the back and let into the garden like two schoolboys let out to play.

"Ergot doesn't grow on flowers," I commented as we passed through the walled fence and into the field.

"No, it does not," Holmes agreed, "but I thought I saw something interesting …" he trailed off, and we waded through the brightly spotted field until we came to the side of the house where stood an odd tree with upside-down little trumpet flowers drooping towards the ground.

"What is that?" I asked.

Holmes pressed a finger to one of the buds, his face furrowed in concentration. "Angel's trumpet, I believe. They are usually native to the South American continent, though it can also grow in China."

"I've never seen it before. What an odd-looking tree."

"It's also called Devil's Breath. When ingested, it can cause a host of symptoms, including a loss of free will. I wasn't expecting this, but it certainly adds shape to the mystery."

He glanced back at the house, noting the curtains closed tightly, and removed the pilfered tea container to look at it closely. He smelled the contents carefully and shook a few leaves into his palm, his face scrunching in both distaste and satisfaction at what he had evidently found.

"Look at this," he directed me, pointing to a small scratch on the side of the container. "I saw the same scratch on one of the tea containers in Mr. Mathews' kitchen. It must be a small defect in the tea caddy. When the container is pulled from it, some imperfection nicks its side. It's an easy enough thing to check. Come, we'll wire Lestrade at the train station."

We sent a telegram for the inspector to meet us in London at the Mathews' townhouse. On the train, I asked Holmes what he found in the tea. He once again shook some of the very fragrant leaves into his hand, and I leaned over as he delicately shifted them with an elegant finger. "Here, that black long grain? That's ergot. But here, also smell this." He offered me a small, dried flower petal.

"It's very musky," I confirmed.

"That's Devil's Breath."

"So ergot and this other poison? But, Holmes, that tree was old. Either he has great foresight, or he conveniently had that poison on hand at his mother's home?"

"Mmmmm," Holmes murmured, deep in thought, "It makes me wonder if another look into the first Mrs. Mathews' death isn't in order as well. I wonder if there was any financial benefit to her passing."

"You think he's done this before? He plans to marry women and then murder them for their life insurance?"

"I don't know if he plans it. But once you get away with a crime, you may be tempted to try your luck twice. His business is failing, he's on the brink of economic humiliation. Perhaps he leaned back on old tricks."

"First, we have to convince Lestrade that he's the villain behind this death."

"That won't be hard. The tea is clearly made to be exchanged without notice. It contains poison. Any amateur chemist could prove that, and I'm no amateur. A confrontation is in order, Watson, and the confrontation is the most exciting part of our work, wouldn't you agree?"

The confrontation ended up being delayed. Our trio was invited into the Mathews' home by a newly hired doorman who, with much more dignity than the housekeeper in Horley, escorted us back into the clean sitting-room. Like before, Holmes waited a brief moment before herding us with stealth into the kitchen.

"Déjà vu," I murmured.

"Eh?" Lestrade queried as we entered the kitchen, doing our best to be quiet. "What is that?"

"It means 'already seen' in French. A philosopher speculated recently that a long-forgotten perception can trigger a feeling a reliving a moment," I explained.

Lestrade chuckled. "Odd. It's usually the other one explaining these intellectual concepts to me."

The 'other one', Holmes, was busy opening the tea caddy. He beckoned Lestrade to him with some impatience and demonstrated that the two containers had identical scratches, fitting perfectly into the tea caddy.

"This one," he held it up, "contains harmless green tea. This one contains multiple poisons that cause hallucinations, compliance, and overall mental deterioration."

Lestrade sighed. "It's always the husband, isn't it?"

"Patterns are patterns for a reason," Holmes confirmed wryly. "Come, let's see what Mr. Mathews has to say for himself." He pushed the caddy and the extra tea container further back on the counter, clearly setting it up for the denouement of the whole affair, and we reentered the sitting-room to await our prey.

Our prey remained elusive. After the clock had ticked by a quarter of an hour, little Maddie once again received us with that restrained grace that I found so admirable.

"My dear," Holmes greeted kindly, "We were expecting to speak to your father."

"I'm afraid he isn't here," she apologized. "A telegram came through about an hour ago, and he left in a hurry."

"He did not tell you where he was going?"

"No, not a word. He seemed very worried." An anxious look crossed her face, and I felt a surge of sympathy for this girl whose recent loss was about to be compounded.

"Do you have the telegram?" Holmes asked eagerly.

"He shoved it into his pocket as he left. Is something the matter?"

He waved off her concern with practiced ease. "No, not at all. Do you mind if we wait for a little longer to see if he returns?"

"Of course. Would you all like something to eat? Some tea?"

Holmes gently took her shoulder and, with a skill that I could never quite understand, managed to herd her towards the door without her realizing she was being herded. "No, no, dear. We have no wish to inconvenience you. Please, feel no need to keep us company."

She looked undecided for a moment before nodding, her tiny hand going to the door handle as if directed by a higher power. That higher power being Holmes, of course. "I'll be just upstairs. If you need me, ring for the doorman."

"Ah, we noticed you have expanded your household."

"Yes, father hired Mr. Hardy yesterday. I predict we'll have a full staff again very soon."

"That will be well for you, to have a lady's-maid and a governess to rely on," I commented gently.

Sadness marred her face, and tears filled her eyes. She blinked them away valiantly. "Yes," she agreed hastily. "Good afternoon, gentlemen."

"Dear heavens, I didn't mean to upset her," I lamented after she had gone.

"I do not think your words have pained her any more than her recent loss, Watson," Holmes reassured.

"Does she have somewhere to go?" Lestrade asked, retaking his seat. "I mean, when this is all said and done, her father will likely get the noose."

"She has an aunt by marriage. I hope she will take her in," I said.

"That telegram was from his mother," Holmes announced, crossing his ankle over his knee. "She must have been sharper than I gave her credit for and wired him that two men were looking about the house. She may have even noticed the missing tea."

"Are you saying she is an accomplice?"

"I wouldn't be surprised," Holmes shrugged. "I'm not so sure how we could prove it."

"So was the trampling merely an accident?" Lestrade asked. "He may have been poisoning her, but I'm not sure what evidence I can bring against him for murder."

Holmes scowled. "He routinely induced her to take mind-altering substances, one of which makes a victim extremely compliant, and likely ordered her to wander outside at a danger to herself. I don't think it mattered much to him exactly how she met her fate, but in that state, time was working against her. A fall, a rough villain in a dark alley, or horses' hooves – in the end, he would have his money and a chance to restart his business. People have gotten hanged for less."

"If he rushed to Horley, we likely passed him on our way back. If he left an hour ago, as Maddie said, we have a bit more of a wait on our hands," I grumbled.

A faltering thud from the other side of the sitting room door drew us all up short.

Holmes stood and flung the door open. Maddie stood at the bottom of the stair, gripping the balustrade with a grip so tight her knuckles were white.

"My dear! What ever is the matter?" Holmes asked.

She pressed a hand to her stomach. "I do not feel well, sirs. I think I may need a doctor."

As a doctor, I moved forward and steadied her. "How are you feeling? What's bothering you?"

She looked very pale. She licked her lips a few times. "I feel sick to my stomach and shaky. I think I may faint."

Holmes circled a supporting arm around her waist as I checked her pupils and pulse, which was beating frantically and erratically. She faltered, only staying upright with our help.

"When did you start feeling this way," I asked, pressing my hand to her forehead to gauge her temperature.

"Just now. I was sitting at my desk, writing, and the room spun." She held out a hand as if she had never seen it before. It was shaking terribly.

Holmes made a sudden grunt, a distressed sound that I had never heard from him before. "Maddie," he asked calmly, though I was familiar enough with him to hear the undercurrent of urgency in his tone, "did you make yourself some tea?"

"Yes, I brought a cup to my room. It tasted funny, but I put more milk in …" she trailed off, swaying.

Panic stabbed at my chest. "Holmes-"

"All right, dear," he interrupted, his voice soothing, "perhaps a brief stop at the hospital may be in order. Don't you agree, Watson?"

I took her other arm as Lestrade hurried outside to fetch a cab. Holmes darted to the kitchen for a moment before returning.

"Am I in trouble?" the young girl wailed, clearly sensing that she was in dire straits.

"No, no, not at all," I replied, guiding her down the hall. "But perhaps a bit of antimony and a few hours of observation are in order."

She followed with a malleable passivity that was troubling. It was fortunate for her that she was in the company of trustworthy men. We bundled her into a cab and headed towards Charing Cross. She put her head against my lapel and lapsed into a dumb silence that I could not break her out of. Her pulse was still racing, and I wondered if she was even aware of what was happening any longer.

"Holmes, will she be all right?" Lestrade whispered.

"She should be. Prolonged use is when it becomes more dangerous, but Watson is right. She should be carefully observed for a few days." He clenched his fist. "I'm such an imbecile," he castigated himself. "I never should have been so offhand with the whole thing while a young lady was in the house. You know I'm fond of the dramatic finale, Watson, but please remind me from now on that it is not the most important consideration."

"Let's not focus on fault," I murmured, "Let's get her seen to."

The waiting-room of Charing Cross was habitually crowded, but upon relating the nature of our predicament to the nurses, the young lady was immediately escorted into the inner room full of curtains and beds. I accompanied her to the private area, removing my coat and helping the nurse administer an emetic, the results of which were always unpleasant.

After the contents of her stomach were expelled. I sat with her for a few moments, monitoring her pulse. She began to stir, asking for water and answering my questions with admirable calm. Once I was relatively sure she was out the woods, I left her to the fine care of the nurses and retreated to the waiting room.

Holmes had disappeared into the administration office and was just retaking his seat when I returned. "I dashed off a telegram to Mathews' home in London and his former home in Horley. I imagine he'll be here soon. I also sent a wire to the aunt in Bristol. I foresee she may be needed soon."

After roughly half an hour, a small-statured, bespectacled doctor approached us, thanking me for my help and reassuring us that the young patient seemed to be doing better, but they wished to keep her for observation for at least a day.

"We aren't her family," I explained as we introduced ourselves. "Her father should be here soon-"

"Speak of the devil, and he shall appear," Holmes murmured, looking over my shoulder.

I turned to see Mathews stalking towards us through the mass of waiting patients.

"What is this?" he demanded of Holmes. "Why are you sending me urgent telegrams about my daughter being ill?" He was red-faced and breathing heavily from his exertions to hurry here. It was clear, at least, that his feelings for his daughter were genuine even if he discarded wives like used napkins.

Holmes held up a conciliatory hand. "Nothing to be alarmed about," he comforted, "she had a bad reaction to something she ingested." He pulled the tea container from his jacket and handed it to Lestrade. "Is there some ingredient in this homemade tea of yours that may have caused an adverse effect?" he asked with exaggerated innocence. "It seems she drank it and immediately felt ill."

Mr. Mathews' eyes had gone wide at the sight of the tea caddy. "Did- did you," he stammered, "did you feed my daughter that tea? Is that my tea from my mother's house? Is that why you were snooping about?"

There was unmistakable accusation in his voice, and Holmes tilted his head with curiosity. "Why do you ask that? Is there something amiss with the tea, sir?"

Mathews threw his hat and coat onto a nearby chair in a fit of anger. "You know good and well, sir, what is in that tea! You dared to give that to my Maddie! You would do that to a child!"

All pretense of innocence fell from the detective's face. He stepped to the fuming man with a piercing gaze. "So you admit that there is something amiss with the tea, sir?"

Mathews looked from Holmes to Lestrade to the tea and back again. It was clear he knew the game was up. I tensed, wondering if he would run or if concern for his daughter would keep him here.

"What is wrong with the tea?" Holmes asked, punctuating each word carefully and forcefully.

Our quarry was well and cornered. I flexed my hands, aware of the whispering spectators surrounding us, viewing our tete-a-tete with concerned fascination. Mathews also seemed to be aware of the many witnesses who had just heard him essentially confess to knowing the tea the inspector held was poisoned. A nurse was standing nearby, in habitual readiness and attention for whatever would follow.

What followed, no one really expected, not even Holmes. Instead of running or slumping in wearied resignation to his fate, Mathews pulled back quickly and delivered an unexpected punch to my friend's face. The detective, in a rare moment of being caught off guard, knocked over a smattering of chairs as he doubled over from the force of the blow.

"That's less than you deserve for poisoning my daughter!" he roared as Lestrade and I rushed forward to restrain him. The few waiting patients nearby had scattered with loud gasps and murmuring, giving the scene a wide berth.

Holmes was bent over, holding the side of his face. Once we had Mathews under control, helped by the irons Lestrade clapped on his wrists, I noticed Holmes shaking.

Both the nurse and I rushed to his side in concern. He stood to his full height, and I saw with relief and some irritation that he was laughing. "By jove!" he declared, "I was not ready for that!" he seemed absolutely delighted to have been struck, wiping the blood from his chin and then gracelessly digging around his mouth until he pulled out a tooth. "The man knocked my canine out," he commented as if it were an exciting surprise.

The nurse tried to lead him away for medical aid, but he brushed her off. "No, no, ma'am. I'm afraid my only hope is a speedy visit to my dentist." He gently shoved the tooth back into its spot, flinching in pain. "Watson, let's be off, eh?" he suggested wryly, his words mumbled by the effort of keeping his tooth in place, "If we do not hurry, this tooth may end up in my box of mementos instead of in my mouth."

"Do you think Mrs. Hudson would allow me to tinker with the bath pipes?"

I sipped at my tea, my attention on the notes in front of me. "What do you mean by 'tinker', Holmes?" I scratched out a name; my list of possible invitees to my upcoming nuptials was painfully short and shrinking as I realized most of the men I used to know were my comrades in the military, and many had not retired to civilian life in or around London. I doubted they would want to make the long travel for an old army friend they had not spoken to in years.

Holmes, for his part, was sprawled out in his chair, dressed but unkempt. Since the Agra case, he had not left the flat, opting instead to indulge in that seven-percent solution at an alarming rate. Even distracted as I was by my wedding plans, I had been looking in vain for something to distract him before the drug finally made irreparable damage to that brilliant mind of his. In only a few days, we would receive that fated visit from Dr. Mortimer that would send us to the foggy moors of Baskerville, but for now, he seemed unbearably bored. Or, perhaps, avoiding the topic of my nuptials.

He shifted his stockinged feet closer to the crackling hearth. The firelight drew attention to the numerous puncture marks and bruises dotting his forearms; his sleeves were rolled up, displaying the evidence of his dismaying activity in the most brazen manner.

"There has been some success in the installation of showering mechanisms in modernized bathrooms," he answered, "and I'm of like mind with many experts that the overhead shower provides a more effective cleaning than a bath."

I set my cup down, giving him an amused look. "You intend to install a shower in Mrs. Hudson's bath?"

He shrugged. The motion was meant to appear idle, but it seemed a forced gesture. "It shouldn't be too difficult."

I turned back to my list. "I didn't realize you were an expert in indoor plumbing."

"As I said, it shouldn't be too difficult." I could feel his darkened gaze on me. I felt a surge of regret.

I tempered my tone. "Perhaps you could draw up some plans," I humoured. "Or find a new case."

He waved a dismissive hand. "Boring. Banal."

"Beneficial," I finished cheerfully. Then, taking a sip of my tea, I muttered under my breath, "Cannot be any more tedious than this."

He heard me. I could feel his glare. "What can compare to a treasure, a wooden-legged men, and poisonous darts, Watson?"

"Lower your standards," I answered tightly.

"Not advice I'm generally willing to heed, in any area of life," Holmes said, bitterly, and then stood, his face suddenly clouded with abstract concentration. "… Perhaps I could sketch out an idea. The existing pipes are new …"

He settled at his writing desk and fell into the quiet work of jotting quick notes on a piece of scrap paper laying nearby. I took a moment to observe him privately, noting the disarray of his hair and the looseness of his undone collar, and silently prayed for a client with a diverting problem to harken our doorstep. Holmes had taken the news of my engagement with neutral grace and had given no indication that it weighed on his mind, but I could not help feel a pang of worry that I was abandoning him to his own, often unhealthy, devices. My friend, for all his solitary intellectualism, did not seem to do well on his own.

"I believe you were completing your guest list, Watson," he interrupted dryly without turning. Damn man must have had eyes on the back of his head. I returned my attention to my task, flushing with embarrassment.

An instant before the doorbell rung, he raised his chin and cocked his head like a cocker spaniel hearing the dinner bell. I cast a silent thank you to the heavens as I heard Mrs. Hudson open the door, leading our unexpected visitor up the stairs after a moment of discussion.

Our long-suffering landlady entered, bearing a card. "A Mrs. Oswald to see you, Mr. Holmes."

To my absolute dismay, he waved his hand irritably. "Tell her I am unavailable."

"No," I stood abruptly. "Send her in," I overrode, doing my best to ignore the look of indignant irritation my companion was levelling at me.

Mrs. Hudson, of the same mind as me as to the recent state of her tenant, obeyed my directive and politely showed in a middle-age woman of graceful carriage and sensitive face. She tugged at her lace gloves, her pretty green eyes shifting from me to my companion as if attempting to decide which of us she was seeking.

Holmes spoke before she was able to introduce herself, "I'm sorry for the confusion, my dear, but my schedule is all full up at the moment." Rudely, he had not even bothered to turn to look at her.

"No, it is not," I said firmly. I gestured her towards the wicker chair. "Have a seat. And my friend will sit here," I said pointedly, patting his chair by the fire, "and listen to your problem."

Holmes's look of disbelief quirked into a wry amusement. He dropped his pen dramatically and padded over the chair and fell into it, stifling a sigh.

I sat, clearing my throat in what I hoped was a subtle warning. In the early days of our arrangement, I may have demurred to Holmes's every mood, but after all these years, I was not above kicking him if he deserved it. I trusted he knew this.

He cleared his own throat, straightening in his chair. "Apologies, madam. Would you like a cup of coffee or tea? I see you've loitered about outside in the cold for some time."

She turned down the offer with a wave of her hand but did not ask him to clarify his observations. I could easily see the dampness of her shoulders spoke of one who had spent some time in the London drizzle after alighting from her cab and before ringing the bell.

"I do not wish to intrude any more upon your valuable time than I need to, Mr. Holmes," she stated politely. If Holmes detected the slight sliver of irony in her tone, he made no indication of it.

"You're here out of concern for a loved one, though this concern has an element of selfishness to it." He paused, considering. "A husband, then."

She nodded. "The matter does concern my husband, who is not aware I have come to see you." She pulled a few folded notes from her small handbag. "My name is Constance Oswald. I married Percival Oswald twenty years ago. We've resided in relative peace with one another in Mayfair. My husband is a complex man. In some ways, he is very vibrant, unrestrained, but in other cases he is extremely reserved." She paused as if expecting a response. Holmes pressed a finger to the bridge of his nose, and I nodded hastily to urge her on, hoping she would quickly come to the point before Holmes's very short patience ebbed entirely.

"My husband is a man of independent wealth. I know nothing of his finances – besides some indication that he invests – and much of his private thoughts are kept from me. He does, however, hold a not so minor position in the government as the Assistant Secretary to Indian Affairs."

"I know of him," Holmes interjected. He gave her a quick, insincere smile. "My brother occupies a very minor role in government, so I have some familiarity."

She nodded, looking flustered at this before continuing, "He believes wholeheartedly in the theory that women must not be burdened with masculine matters." A flutter of exasperation crossed her elegant brow. "Nay, he believes women cannot understand masculine matters. This often forces me to, excuse my frankness, snoop if I wish to know anything that happens under my own roof. It was in the course of this snooping that I found these."

She held out her folded notes. Holmes did not accept them, so I took them from her, shuffling through them.

"What do they contain?" he asked instead, languidly.

"I believe my husband is being blackmailed. The notes speak of his 'secret' and make numerous requests for money to be left at different areas in town." She looked expectantly at me. I obediently skimmed one correspondence and hummed.

"Yes," I corroborated, "do you know if your husband has entertained any of these demands?"

"I'm afraid I do not. I can hardly ask him."

Holmes stood suddenly, taking the notes from me and passing them back to our guest. His movements were not rude or abrupt, but he was decidedly brusque.

"I'm sorry, madam. I cannot help you with your problem. I advise you to simply ask your husband and accept his answer."

"Sir-" she started as my companion turned away.

"Holmes," I began but he cut me off with a sharp glance.

"I cannot help you with your problem," he stated firmly in a voice that brooked no argument, even from me, "I apologize as I see you are greatly distraught, but this is not a matter I specialize in."

She glanced at me for aid, but seeing my own hopeless look, she stood and inclined her chin frostily. "I am sorry for bothering you, sir." She separated one letter from the rest and handed it to me. "In case your busy schedule clears, perhaps you could be bothered to take a cursory glance over it," she explained and then left in a rustle of skirts.

"Holmes!" I exclaimed once the door had closed behind her. "How absurdly discourteous of you!"

He picked up his violin and forestalled my remonstration with a loud screech of the bow against the cords. He tucked the thing under his chin and rolled his eyes at me.

"No amount of boredom will induce me to get involved in trite romantic affairs of this city's denizens. Clearly, the letters were written by a former mistress demanding money from Mr. Oswald in exchange for her silence. I am honestly shocked the clearly intelligent Mrs. Oswald has not already figured this out. I would think it would be a woman's first thought." He played a few low, melancholic notes. "I do not chase down missing love letters or spy on philandering men."

"He does work for the government, Holmes. It would not be out of the realm of possibility that this is a matter of political-"

"No, the letters ask for money. There is no political inclinations reflected there. In my experience, the most common behavior gentlemen regularly engage in while desperately pretending they do not is adultery."

"You could have very well taken a moment to tell her that. Without payment, you would have been doing a kindness, not work," I reprimanded firmly, sitting back down at the dining table.

"Would that have been a kindness?" he answered.

I could not think of a sufficient response, so I dug back into my now cold tea and crossed a few more names from my list, resolved to put the whole encounter from my mind.

Holmes fiddled on his violin, all thoughts of indoor showers apparently forgotten. He droned upon the thing for half an hour, but upon striking a bad note more than once, he flung the treasured instrument down and paced in front of the fire.

I ignored him the best I could, keeping track of his movements from the corner of my eye. I had meant to ask him to serve as best man at my wedding, but in his current state, I could not risk spoiling the moment. I was also worried he would decline my request, and I am not sure how our friendship would proceed in the face of such a rejection.

He stopped and idly picked up the letter Mrs. Oswald had left, unfolding it and reading it quickly.

He stood, looking at the letter for a long while, a chagrined expression slowly transforming his face. "Well, Watson," he said at last, "mark this day and time for I am about to say something I rarely say, much to your everlasting frustration."

I set my teacup down. "And what is that?"

"I believe I was wrong."

My eyebrows shot up into my hairline. I scrabbled for the small notepad in my jacket pocket and made a show of jotting down the time.

Holmes let out an irritated grunt and took the three steps that brought him close enough to wiggle the paper in my face.

"This is not a woman's hand, doctor." He explained and waited for me to get my humour under control. I took the paper from him and peered closely at it.

"Notice the surety of the t's and I's."

"Mmhhmm," I agreed despite my complete ignorance as to what I was meant to notice.

He snatched the thing from me, the first spark of excited interest lighting up his grey eyes. He went back to the fire and examined the thing minutely in the glow of the flames, smelling the paper and running his fingers over the corners and edges. He knelt down and tilted it towards the flames until you could nearly see through the material before letting it hang listlessly from his fingertips and gazing into the flames, his thoughts turned inwards.

I knew Holmes had made an exhaustive study of any and everything that could be used to trace someone: clay, tobacco, shoes, clothing, ink, stamps, and, yes, stationary. I could imagine that strange mind of his rifling through his brain attic of carefully collected information for what he sought.

After a moment, he stood and slid the letter into his waistcoat pocket and disappeared into his rooms, reemerging minutes later looking pristinely put together in a dark blue frock coat, his collar straightened, and his hair neatly brushed back.

Snatching his hat from the rack, he left without a backward glance or even an acknowledgment of my existence, leaving me alone with my pitiful, short list of friends and a question dying on my lips.

When he returned, his expression lacked that bright gleam of excitement that so often accompanied a fascinating problem, but he looked satisfied.

I had already eaten dinner and had settled into my chair with the evening *Times*. "You look like a man who found what he was looking for," I commented, folding my paper away.

He packed his pipe and sat in the chair opposite me. "Indeed. While this was certainly not the thorniest case I've ever encountered, it was a pleasant, albeit brief, distraction. I was able to track the stationary to a printer near Evesham. From there, I was led to a small barristers' office. They were accommodating enough to speak to me and informed me that one of their colleagues had not been to work in the last two days. It was simple work to compare the handwriting on the letter to that of some correspondence on his desk. Our blackmailer is Michael Everett. Thirty years old, unmarried, and, by all accounts, usually reliable."

"Did you acquire an address?"

"I did, but I was informed that there have been unsuccessful efforts to reach him there. It may be a simple matter to station myself nearby and watch his house to see if he comes or goes, but the very pleasant and talkative secretary described Mr. Everett to me as a dashing tall man with blonde hair and as the most devote Catholic who can be found every Sunday at St. Andrews for confession, come hell or high water – a fitting idiom, in this case – so it seems this would be the most efficient avenue to pursue."

"You mean to waylay a man at church?"

"I said nothing of waylaying him," he protested, but there was a mischievous gleam in his eye. "But knowing when and where a man will be makes it an easy thing to arrange a meeting."

Sunday morning, I awoke to find Holmes already gone, a brief note commanding I wait for him outside of St. Andrews at noon left on the mantle.

I had no other pressing engagements until I was to meet Mary for dinner at six, so I dressed and hurried to make the appointment.

St. Andrews was a small church near SoHo and blessedly quiet even on a Sunday. I mounted the steps and entered the auditorium. Statues of the crucified Messiah bore down on me ominously. A small empty pulpit and a priest's double curtained confessional stood at the front of the pews. The only other occupant of the darkened room was the priest; I could hear the shuffle of his shoes in his designated booth. He did not come out to meet me, and I sat gently on the front pew bench and looked up at the beautiful stained glass window filtering the grey sunlight into the room in muted, pleasing colors.

I wasn't Catholic. Indeed, I was a Protestant only by name. My time in Afghanistan had caused some definite disillusionment about our place in the world. I often wondered if there was truly any higher power out there, and if so, how could such horrors as I had seen on the battlefield of Maiwand be permitted?

My upcoming nuptials with Mary had certainly renewed some of my faith in the innate goodness of the world, but I could not think of that without an accompanying pang of regret about leaving my flatmate to his own devices, all alone right after Christmas season.

The rustle of movement in the centre compartment reminded me that I was not alone. Feeling a bit awkward, I rose and stepped over to the confessional, wondering if I wasn't committing some sin by stepping in when I did not practice this faith.

I was not going to kneel, so I sat, barely able to make out the form of the priest through the lattice barrier.

I said nothing at first, feeling suddenly lost as to what I was doing. On the other side of the booth, the priest shifted and then, appearing to realize I was not going to start, murmured kindly, "May God, who has enlightened every heart, help you to know your sins and trust in His mercy. Do you have a confession to make?"

"As unorthodox as it is, father, I am not Catholic. Are we allowed to speak?"

"Of course, son. Is there something you need to confide?"

I sighed, leaning back, feeling a bit more comfortable at how kind the man sounded. "I'm not sure. I have done nothing sinful, but there are some things I feel guilty about."

"Mmhhmm?"

"I will be married early next year."

There was a heavy pause. The priest's voice was benevolent but sure when he spoke again. "Is this a wedding of necessity?"

"No, no." I clarified quickly. "You see, I live with a good friend of mine, and I'm afraid I'm leaving him quite abruptly."

The priest took a deep breath, giving my words serious contemplation. "Surely," he started, "this is the way of the world. Your friend must understand."

"He does. He claims he does. But his behavior is becoming more worrisome."

"What behavior?"

I had no desire to speak in detail of the detective's personal habits, even in the safety of a confessional booth. Instead, I answered obliquely, "I do not think he does well on his own."

"Perhaps you could help find him his own wife to be his companion?"

I stuttered. "I don't think that's a feasible avenue-"

"Why not? Is your friend terribly hideous?"

"No, indeed not-" I stammered, flustered at the odd direction this conversation had taken. Then I felt an angry flush flare up my face, and I banged out of the confessional loudly, forgetting for a moment that we were in a house of worship.

I swung open the door to the priest's compartment. Holmes, dressed in a full priest cassock, smirked up at me, unrestrained glee dancing in his light eyes.

I pressed my fingers to the bridge of my nose.

"You forgot to say 'forgive me, father, for I have sinned', Watson. Don't you know your rite of confession?" he asked with mock solemnity.

"Holmes, I will strike you."

He gave me a look of exaggerated shock. "We're in a church, Watson!" He laughed and stood, sidling by me with no appearance of trepidation in the face of my anger.

"Why do you even have a cassock?" I demanded. "You're not allowed to pretend to be a priest."

He waved his hand like he was swatting away a fly. "There is no law against impersonating a priest or cleric of any church. At least, as long as I'm not attempting to marry someone."

"There may be no man-made laws, but the sacrilege!"

"You're not even Catholic, Watson," he laughed.

"You did that on purpose strictly to embarrass me," I accused

"I did nothing of the sort," he protested, failing to restrain his delight. "I had no idea you'd enter confessional. Especially since I had clearly told you to wait outside. *Especially* since, as we have both already pointed out, you are not Catholic."

"What if another priest had been in here?"

"We're between services. Everett did not attend this morning, evidently trying to lay low for some reason. I hope he will slide in during this period of inactivity."

As if on cue, the main door began to creak open. Holmes pushed me suddenly towards the curtained wall near the confessional. "Quick, man, hide."

I floundered but allowed myself to be ungracefully deposited in the hiding place. I heard Holmes reenter the confession box. Through a small gap in the curtain, I could see the figure entering the church.

He was a tall man, slightly taller than me but not as tall as Holmes. He had a robust, sportsman's figure, and sandy hair. He was quite handsome, of the sort many women would pay attention to.

Belying these natural gifts, he walked with timid, nearly hunched steps, stopping for a moment in the aisle as if expecting a full church before seeming to shake himself and making his way to the confessional. As he drew close, I steadied my breathing, frightened of being caught out. I heard him kneel on his knees.

I felt a flush of shame. Here I had scolded Holmes for the sacrilege of impersonating a priest, and yet I was now hiding, fully intent to eavesdrop on a man's private confession. I could hardly step out now, however. For not the first or last time in my long relationship with Holmes, I inwardly cursed the detective and my apparent inability to disobey him. Knowing that it was Holmes there and not an authentic priest caused me to send up my own prayer, hoping we could be forgiven this transgression.

From my vantage point, I could hear their conversation clearly:

Unlike me, Mr. Everett began, "In the name of the Father, and of the Son, and of the Holy Spirit. Amen."

Holmes clear voice, gentle and nearly fatherly came through: "May God, who has enlightened every heart, help you to know your sins and trust in His mercy," he repeated and I wondered where he had learned this script.

"Bess me, Father, for I have sinned. It has been a week since my last confession. These are my sins ..." Instead of enumerating them, he fell silent. Holmes shifted. Because I knew him, I understood it was impatience. He was obviously hoping this man would confess to attempted blackmail, and the silence that hung was creating no shortage of anticipation.

Finally, my friend prompted, his voice restrained, "What sins have you to confess, son?"

"The woman I love died, and I caused it."

I startled. Even through the walls of the booth, I could sense Holmes too had not been expecting this declaration.

When he spoke again, there was an edge of restlessness to his voice. "Are you confessing to taking someone's life?" he asked carefully.

"Not directly, father. But my actions caused events that I believe led to Jeanette's murder-" the man broke off, stifling a sob.

Holmes cleared his throat. I suspected he had not prepared for this and was struggling to know what a real priest would say in such a situation. A misstep could mean his game was up, and dealing with the fall out of his little pantomime may prove humiliating.

"What actions may that be, son?"

"I threatened someone, and I suspect they thought it was her."

"What was the nature of this threat?"

"It does not matter," he said hurriedly. "I am sorry for these and all of my sins. My God, I am sorry for my sins with all my heart," he recited. "In choosing to do wrong and failing to do good, I have sinned against you whom I should love above all things. I firmly intend, with your help to do penance, to sin no more, and to avoid whatever leads me to sin. My God, have mercy." He stopped, and the silence that followed was awkward, expectant.

At last, Holmes seemed to realize he could push no more without drawing attention to himself. He ran through the absolution quickly, but our heartbroken and guilt-ridden confessor did not seem to notice.

The man nearly ran from the confessional once he was dismissed, and I waited until his footsteps receded before quietly removing myself from my hiding place.

Holmes opened the confessional door and came out looking sober and unsettled.

"Holmes," I murmured with a sort of horrified awe, "you just absolved a man of his sins."

"Not the worst act I've ever committed," he replied absently. He rubbed his chin. "These are deeper waters than I suspected. Yet another rare event –

something occurring that I did not at all anticipate."

"It's easy enough to put together," I commented. "Everett penned those letters threatening to expose some aspect of Mr. Oswald's past in connection to this Jeanette, and he believes Mr. Oswald assumed the notes originated from her and killed her."

Holmes arched an eyebrow but did not argue with me. "Deeper waters, indeed. Most likely, Jeanette was a former mistress."

"Should we take this to Lestrade?"

Holmes nodded but appeared distracted. "At least he may be able to give us some information about this unfortunate woman. Our speculation is all fine and dandy, but I'd prefer some evidence as well."

He stripped off his cassock and folded it carelessly on a pew, reaching under the seat and pulling out his own frock coat and tie.

At my questioning look, he clarified. "This is not my garb, Watson. I've yet to add priest to my wardrobe of costumes."

"You stole a priest cassock?"

"Borrowed. And now it will be found and all is well. Come, to Lestrade."

Lestrade was not happy to see us. The Metropolitan Police were feeling the after-effects of the Ripper killings, and the shake-ups happening at the higher levels of office were trickling down to the inspectors and the men on the beat. Our colleague and occasional friend looked haggard and harried, and the sight of us in his office doorway seemed to aggravate rather than alleviate his stress.

He rolled his eyes heavenwards. "For the love of all that is holy, please, not now, Mr. Holmes. I have not called for you. I have no need of you. I have no time for you."

Holmes entered his office and swept into a chair without being invited. "I have need of you, Lestrade."

"Well, if the great Sherlock Holmes has need of something, we must tend to it immediately," he said dryly, dropping his pen and leaning back wearily in his chair.

Holmes observed him, taking in everything in that quick way of his.

"Buck up, Lestrade," he said cheerfully, "I may be able to assist you, actually, in what I suspect is an unsolved murder."

Lestrade gestured irritably to a large stack of files on his desk. "I have plenty of those, Mr. Holmes."

I could tell it took great forbearance for Holmes to restrain himself from making a jesting, derogatory comment. When he was very young, he would have lacked the wisdom of silence when faced with a clear opportunity to make a dig at the inspector. Age, and I believe very real affection for Lestrade, had taught him to occasionally hold his tongue.

"Well, we are interested in a particular one. A woman who goes by 'Jeanette'. We have no last name."

Lestrade thought for a moment before sighing and digging through the pile. "We do have a case with a woman of that name. Jeanette White." He rifled through the file pages after he freed it from the mess. "Performer who lived in a neat but cheap row of flats near Convent Garden. Twenty-five years of age, unmarried. She was strangled. It seems clear the intruder entered and exited her rooms through a window with a lock that had been broken."

"Motive?"

"None that we can find. No one had any complaint against the girl. We suspect someone passing by saw her, took a fancy, perhaps meant to cause her some mischief. Things went awry, she fought back, and lost her life for her troubles." He tossed down the file. "Other than that, we have no leads."

Holmes cast a nonchalant glance around at the whirlwind of papers. "Your office is a bit closed in, inspector. Fancy some fresh air?"

Lestrade leaned back. "If I say no, you'll simply break into her flat, won't you?"

"Yes."

He frowned. "Why does this interest you, Holmes? There is nothing unique about this case at all." His face cleared with recognition. "Or is there? What do you know?"

"Speculation, only," Holmes demurred and stood, clearly expecting us to follow. As usual, we did. Lestrade shook on his coat with no shortage of overt exasperation.

"You better make this worth my time, young man," he warned, but it lacked any real heat.

"Always, Lestrade. Always," Holmes declared, already striding down the hall.

Lestrade let us into the tiny, one-story flat. The front room faced the street, affording its previous occupant with a nice little view of the people coming and going to the small shops that lined the main thoroughfare. Her little bedroom tucked up against the alley, and a half-kitchen completed the amenities. It was not the worst of living spaces, but it was clear whoever resided here was not well-off. Indeed, a young single woman on her own, without the benefits of family wealth, could unfortunately not expect much more.

Holmes stood examining the front door for quite some time. "You say you believe the killer came through the window. Was the door locked when you arrived?"

Lestrade nodded. "Yes, and, at least to me, it appeared that it had not been picked."

Holmes leaned down and took some time examining this for himself. When he stood, he nodded as if satisfied.

"May I see the report?" he held out a scarred hand, and Lestrade passed him the papers from his coat.

He read through them carefully, glancing up now and then as if searching for some item referenced. When he handed them back to Lestrade, he looked annoyed.

"There is no mention of the removal of shoes or the fact that the killer turned off the stove."

"I beg your pardon?"

Holmes pointed at the scratched wood near the doorway. "Our intruder removed his shoes – I say 'his' because they are clearly a man's dress shoes – and proceeded into the house on stockinged feet." He strode into the kitchen, where the remains of a half-cooked dinner still remained, drawing the attention of flies. "Did it not also strike you as odd that she was evidently murdered while cooking, yet the stove was off and the food did not catch fire?"

Lestrade looked a bit flustered. "I didn't pay it much mind, Holmes. She could have turned off the stove when she heard a noise."

Holmes shook his head dismissively but said no more, going to the bedroom and bending down to look closely at the window's broken lock. He opened the window and then closed it, clearly listening for what sound it made. It was loud, scraping in its old metal railing.

Satisfied with that, he stepped back and took in the small table sat next to it, knocked slightly askew, its little vase of now dead flowers tipped to the side.

He narrowed his eyes and then opened the window again, pushing his head out into the alley.

"Someone stood here."

Lestrade and I leaned over. Outside were some pallets and a few discarded sheets of work canvas. A clear circle had been cleared right beneath the window. Lestrade nodded. "I can see that. But that aligns with our report, Holmes. The intruder obviously entered through the unlocked window. There is no other way to enter the flat."

"How did this intruder get to the front door to remove his shoes while leaving no trace of footprints or dirt anywhere in his wake?"

"Maybe he was careful."

"If he were careful he would have removed his shoes here, not traipse through two rooms to do so."

"We only have your speculation that he removed his shoes at all."

Holmes hummed but let the comment pass as if unworthy of his attention. "This lock has been broken for months, but no one entered or exited here." He bent down and looked closely at the sill with his magnifying glass. "No scrapes that would indicate shoes. Though there is an odd scratch here." He dug around in it with a pair of tweezers. "Looks like metal chipped off in the ridge, as if a heavy metal object was slid over the wood. Unfortunately, not enough here for any further analysis."

"How do you know that he did not exit by the window, Holmes? The table here is knocked askew," Lestrade asked, irritated.

"The table could very well have been knocked askew at any time. The key is not that it is askew but that it is not askew enough to allow an adult to lift themselves over the window sill without knocking it completely over."

"Now-"

"Attempt it. Go on, try to lift your leg over the windowsill without hitting the table, Lestrade."

Lestrade did not attempt it. He gave Holmes a witheringly dark glare and tapped his stubbed pencil against his small notepad. After a strained silence, Holmes slid his hands into his pockets and spun around to cross towards the unmade bed. Lestrade made an annoyed clucking sound with his tongue and continued. "Well, then. I guess, therefore, the murderer entered through the front door. Unless, of course, you mean to reveal that he dug an underground mine underneath the flat and came up under her bed in some elaborate plot."

"You do know I adore an elaborate plot, but alas-" the detective dropped down and peered under the bed in a sprightly move meant entirely to chafe at the inspector. "No, there is no mine here." He stood and spun on his heel, pretending not to notice – or relish – Lestrade's exasperation.

"However," he continued, "if our man entered through the front door, which was locked, then he is either a master lock pick, which I doubt – there is literally no sign of tampering – or he knew Miss Jeanette White. That would mean this was not a random act of opportunity, but premeditated murder by someone who knew her. But I suspect you already suspect that, do you not, Lestrade?"

Lestrade tapped his pencil again. "I may have wondered the same thing myself, but I have little evidence to support my theories. You may feel free to speculate, Mr. Holmes, but need I remind you that I work in an official capacity and must therefore base my theories on concrete facts."

Holmes hummed again and wandered into the kitchen. I followed him into the main room and glanced around. It always felt odd to be in someone's home after their death, surrounded by items that spoke of their life.

Miss White was clearly a curious girl. Her home was a bit untidy but overall clean, filled with items that spoke of her interests. A small bookshelf filled with fiction, a table with an old but clearly well-maintained Victrola and scattered music sheets. Above her small fireplace mantle, was a pretty watercolor painting that I knew at a glance was worth very little. On the mantle itself were various figurines and dried flowers. On the end was a strange, quirky little alarm clock – a posing skeleton leaning on two bells. I imagined when it rang, it made the skeleton dance. A smile pulled at my lips. What an interesting girl she must have been. I felt a pang of regret that I would never get to meet her.

Holmes interrupted my thoughts, addressing Lestrade. "Your report said that because of the delay in discovering the body, rigor mortis could only provide us with a wide window of possible time of death. But in your report, you also mention that she must have died after eight o'clock at night, but before ten."

"The next door neighbor heard her singing at approximately eight."

"Singing?"

"She was an actress, apparently favored musical theater. The woman next door said she could often hear her in here singing to herself. That narrowed it down a bit. The coroner is certain she was killed before ten o'clock."

"Therefore, we have a two hour window," Holmes said under his breath. "You've been enormously helpful, Lestrade," he announced, starting for the door.

"Holmes," the inspector said tiredly. "At least tell me that you will pass along your conclusions at some point."

Holmes looked affronted. "Of course, and grant you full credit, inspector, as I so often do." For the first time in our relationship with Lestrade, I noticed a sliver of actual hurt in my friend's tone. I was certain Lestrade was not perceptive enough to sense it, but his tone softened, and I quickly rethought my assumption.

"And I'm forever grateful for that, Holmes. But while the way you flutter about, keeping everything so close to the vest, may be exciting for you, it has caused me no shortage of grey hairs."

"Vibrant description, but at least in this case, I am only keeping mum because I do not have all the facts. You would never let me hear the end of it if I was caught in a mistake," he laughed. He tipped his hat in farewell, and we were out of the door.

"Where are we going?" I asked as we regained the kerb.

"The Oswalds."

"You're going to confront him?"

"I haven't made up my mind. I was not lying to Lestrade; I wish to have all the facts before I go off at half-cock accusing others of murder."

The Oswalds lived in a very nice three-story townhouse in Mayfair. We passed the butler our card and were promptly escorted into the drawing room.

It was a cluttered but large room. Mrs. Oswald had clearly been at some knitting, there was a pile of it on her chair. On the comfortable divan was a plump calico that stared at us with wide, black eyes, sniffing us out for danger. A roaring fire was in the hearth, and next to the large French doors looking out to the manicured back garden was a birdcage with a pretty blue and green parrot bobbing happily on its perch. The delicate nameplate on the front of the cage said *Bella*.

Mrs. Oswald took our hands warmly, clasping my friend's for a bit longer in lieu of effusive thanks for reconsidering her plight.

"Gentlemen," she welcomed. "While I am pleased you've taken in interest in my concern, I was not expecting you." She looked a little worried, and I wondered if Holmes had not made an uncharacteristic misstep by coming here where her husband may see us.

Holmes glanced around the room, taking in all the details, and then cutting to the heart of the matter in that brusque but at times refreshing way of his, "Is your husband home at the moment?"

She nodded a bit nervously. "He is. I thought it was clear that I wished this matter to stay between us."

"I thought he was normally at his club at this time?" Holmes asked frowning.

Mrs. Oswald and I startled, surprised that Holmes's interest had evidently extended that far. I wondered when he had time to look into the man's usual schedule.

"He was feeling a bit under the weather," she explained.

"We'll be quick then. I hope you'll pardon us for asking, but where was your husband on Thursday night between roughly eight and ten in the evening?"

She peered intently at him, as if trying to discern the reasoning behind such an inquiry. "We were at the opera. It started at seven and then we went to dinner afterwards. We weren't home until well after midnight."

"You're certain?"

"I'm quite certain, Mr. Holmes." She gave me an amused, questioning glance.

"And there is no way you could be mistaken about the time?" he pressed.

She glanced at me again, as if worried she was failing some sort of test. "I remember where I was, Mr. Holmes. It's hardly a thing to get confused about."

"Of course," Holmes reassured, his smile tight, "it's just that this information complicates some things." He and I shared a meaningful look which our quick hostess noticed. Before she could ask about it, she seemed to hear something in the hall and straightened up perceptibly as the drawing room door opened, revealing a short stout man with a wide, expressive face.

He smiled broadly at us, a pleasant and playful light dancing in his eyes. "Constance, you must tell me we have guests! I could have barreled in here and embarrassed myself!"

Mrs. Oswald laughed, though it rang a bit forced.

"Forgive me, Percy. I was not expecting guests, actually. This is Sherlock Holmes and Doctor John Watson."

"Mr. Sherlock Holmes? The consulting detective? I read about your adventure in *Beeton's*. You are mentioned often in the papers, as well," he exclaimed excitedly, shaking our hands firmly. "I have also made the memorable acquaintance of your brother. To what do we owe the great honor of your presence?" He put a companionable arm around his wife. "I hope we have not been connected to some vile plot."

"No, not any serious business, sir. We are sorry for intruding," Holmes said pleasantly, clearly looking for an excuse to take his leave.

"I don't imagine Sherlock Holmes finds himself engaged often in trivial matters," our host pressed, squeezing his wife's shoulders.

Mrs. Oswald broke in deftly. "I left my gloves at the opera house and, as unlikely as it seems, these two famous gentleman happened to find them. They very kindly returned them to me. Tell me, doctor, how did you like *Manon?*"

I had no idea what *Manon* was and wondered what would have led the woman to think, between the two of us, why I would be the one to help plaster over her lie and not Holmes.

Holmes interjected smoothly, saving me, "Charming, though I see why it was banned for some time."

"I did not care for it. It seems an easy thing to put a woman in her place, and yet I had to endure nearly two hours of lovesick men being run around by a woman infatuated with glitter and gold," Mr. Oswald complained happily.

"Of course," my friend said with false agreeableness. "I prefer Massanet's *Werther.* We are very sorry to have come unannounced. Good day, madam."

"Thank you again, gentlemen. Have a lovely night," Mrs. Oswald said as she shrugged off her husband's embrace and showed us to the door. She made brief, but meaningful eye contact with Holmes as he tipped his hat to her, and we stopped at the front door while Holmes passed the butler a hastily scribbled note.

"Would you please give this to your mistress? With discretion."

The butler seemed to understand our intent and with that practiced neutrality of one of his station, he nodded and slipped the thing into his pocket.

"'Complicates' seems an understatement, Holmes," I commented when we were well away from the doorstep. "The man could not have killed Miss White if he was sitting comfortably at the opera when she died."

Holmes pressed his fingers together under his chin, looking contemplative. "Indeed. You see now why I refrained from telling Lestrade our theory. A clear spanner in the works."

"Could he have hired someone to do the dark deed?"

Holmes sighed, shaking his head. "It's possible, but I can't imagine a man so averse to being blackmailed involving another party in his crimes."

"But we are sure it was him?" I asked tentatively.

Holmes nodded but, in truth, seemed slightly unsure.

As we strode down the darkened street, Holmes glanced at his pocket watch, arching an eyebrow. "You are late."

"I beg your pardon?"

"Aren't you meant to meet Mary at six? It's five past."

"Oh, good lord!" I exclaimed, panicked.

Holmes stepped into the street and masterfully fetched a cab for me. He urged me in. "Go on, old man, hurry. Give Mary my love and sincere apologies in holding you captive."

In the morning, at half past nine, he received a telegram from Mrs. Oswald. After an obligatory tap on his door, I entered, jostling his shoulder and waking him. He looked sleepily up at me until I passed him the missive.

He sat up, eager, reading it quickly.

"What is it?" I asked as he swung his covers off and rose.

"We are to meet Mrs. Oswald at her home between eleven and one tomorrow."

"I am to assume that is when her husband will be out?"

"Capital observation, Watson. Indeed. In the interim, I wish to speak to Lestrade's witnesses to see if some clue was overlooked. That window interests me. Specifically, whatever was passed through it."

We found ourselves picking our way back into the flat. Holmes spent more time at said window. This time, he left and came around the alley, standing in the cleared circle and reaching inwards as if testing his reach towards the little round table nearby. Seemingly satisfied, he came back around and joined me in poor Miss White's old bedroom, giving the table a more thorough examination but, from the frown creasing his brow, I could tell he had found nothing new.

He did a quick survey of the main room. He fiddled with the peculiar little alarm clock that had caught my eye but led me back into the hall, carefully relocking the door behind him.

We slid down the hall to the next flat, tapping loudly on the green door. After a moment, it creaked open and an older woman peered out. I guessed her age to be a little over 60. She squinted at us. I could see from the faint indents on the bridge of her nose that she was missing her usual spectacles.

"Aye?" she asked, a bit distrustfully.

"Good day, madam," Holmes said gallantly. "My name is Sherlock Holmes, and this is my good friend Doctor Watson. We're making inquiries about your former neighbor."

She opened the door wider. "Sherlock Holmes? The detective? Are you here to finally find who hurt poor Jeannie?"

Holmes clasped his gloved hands together and nodded solemnly. "I am. Were you close to Miss White?"

"She was such a sweet girl," she lamented softly. "I believe she was meant to be married soon; she made some coy remarks to me about it, and I met her young man a few times."

"Before that young man, did she have any other suitors?"

"Not that I know of. I've only been living here for five months, in any case."

Holmes nodded in understanding. "Of course. You told the constables that you heard her singing at eight o'clock the night she died, is that correct?"

"Yes, the walls between our flats are a bit thin," she explained.

"Was she in the habit of singing?"

"Oh, all the time. She had some success in minor musicals, but she had aspirations of becoming an opera singer. Her voice was delightful."

"Did you notice anything odd about her singing that night?"

"Odd? Not particularly. She did not sing for very long, perhaps only a few seconds."

"Did you hear anything else around that time?" I interjected.

110

"I don't believe so. I was not paying rapt attention, however."

"Did you see her or anyone else enter or exit the flat?" my friend asked.

"I did not, but I was not looking. The only other thing I remember is that she was cooking at about five o'clock. I could smell the spices she liked to use in her food."

"Five o'clock?" Holmes looked sharply at her. "That may help, ma'am."

"Oh, I don't see how it does, but I sincerely hope so. She didn't deserve what happened to her. Wait here a minute, dear." She walked back into her small flat, leaving the door cracked open, and returned a second later with a small palm-sized cabinet photograph. She handed it to Holmes. "This is Jeanette," she told us. "See how sweet she was?"

Holmes angled the photograph towards me. A very pretty girl with black curly hair smiled back at me. I felt a pang at how young and happy she looked.

Holmes fiddled with the thing for a few moments; he gave no outside indication of it, but I could sense he was slightly uncomfortable. He passed it back solemnly. "She was a very lovely woman," he commented.

She nodded sadly. "I hope you discover whoever did this to her."

We asked a few other flats, but most denied any knowledge of Miss White's comings and goings and saw and heard nothing unusual. One young man, however, who told us he was working from seven o'clock in the evening to one o'clock in the morning, informed us he saw a man turn into the alley as he approached the building's steps on his way home from work. He estimated the time to be close to two o'clock.

"Was he coming from inside the flats?" Holmes asked.

"I couldn't be sure, sir. I really only noticed him because he was dressed nicely. I wondered why someone like that would be skulking down the alley at that time at night. Or morning, rather."

"Did you notice his face?"

"No, he had a scarf pulled up over his mouth and nose. He was a bit on the short side, but that's all I can tell you. I was tired from my work at the factory and was simply eager to get into my bed."

Holmes fell into deep thought for a moment. The young man, looking drained and confused, glanced questioningly at me.

Finally, my friend spoke, "Was he carrying a heavy object?"

"No, nothing."

Holmes, nearly vibrating with excitement, pressed a grateful hand to the man's shoulder. "You have helped me immensely."

He would say no more, settling back in the carriage and closing his eyes. I knew he was not resting, but shifting and organizing the details in his mind until the sequence of events came into relief.

When we reentered our rooms, I was surprised to see Mr. Everett of the infamous confessional booth debacle waiting for us with a warm cup of tea by the hearth. I flushed, embarrassed.

Holmes did not seem surprised and, to my everlasting relief, our guest did not seem to recognize my friend as his counterfeit priest.

He rose and shook the detective's hand. "I must admit I was a bit startled by your summons, sir. I imagine I know what this is all about, however."

Holmes gestured for him to retake his seat and stretched out in his own. "I would think so," he commended, "I take it your life must have been relatively mundane until recently ... my condolences on your loss."

Mr. Everett seemed just barely able to hold back his emotions. He merely nodded, clearing his throat. "I guess I should ask how I came to your attention?"

"It was a simple thing once I was in possession of one of your letters."

"Yes. Quite a foolish thing I did there." He paused and then continued curiously, "Who showed you the letters?" Then, with more outraged anger in his tone, demanded, "Did the blackguard actually come to you for help?"

Holmes remained impassive. "I assume you mean Mr. Oswald, and, no, he is not my client. His wife found your blackmail material and brought it to me. Why did you target Mr. Oswald?"

The man put his teacup down on the table between the armchairs, sighing. "Simple. Jeannie told me about her ... past ... with Mr. Oswald. He had tricked her – she hadn't known he was married, and she believed he loved her. When she found out she was being used, she broke things off. She claimed to hold no real ill-feelings for him and wished to put the entire thing behind her."

"But you did not?"

A blush of shame spread up his face. "I'm not a rich man," he admitted. "I wanted to provide for her. At least, give her a wedding she deserved. I knew he was a wealthy man and a man whose reputation was important to him because of his connection to the government."

"So you thought blackmailing Mr. Oswald was an easy way to gather some coin."

"I did. I never thought it would result in her death."

Holmes lit a cigarette and tilted his chin at our heartbroken visitor. "So you believe her killer is Mr. Oswald?"

"I do," the answer was firm, steely with rage. "But there is no way for me to prove it. I can produce some letters, but that may not be sufficient, and all it would do is ruin me as well."

Holmes leaned back, pulling contentedly on his smoke and observing the man through narrowed eyes. At last, he knocked the ash out into the fireplace and began, his voice carefully measured. "As a general rule, I am not fond of blackmailers. You take a person's moments of weakness and dig into them, twisting, until your victim is bled dry. However, with the full picture in front of me, I see your crime is the lesser of evils. I will try my best not to expose you. But I make no guarantee."

Everett swung his hand sharply through the air with barely restrained excitement. "Oh, as long as you bring that man to the gallows, Mr. Holmes, I do not care what becomes of me."

"Splendid!" Holmes declared cheerily. "Now, I'm close to cornering our villain. I will send word to you as soon as I can." He stood, a clear sign that our meeting was over. Everett understood, standing and letting himself be bustled out of the door.

"I will do anything to help," he assured as he swung on his coat.

Holmes clapped him on the back, using the gesture to gently guide him over the threshold. "I'm glad to hear it. Good day."

He spun around once the door was closed, his eyes twinkling.

"Holmes," I admonished, "that was a bit rude."

He waved his hand dismissively, "He'll be all right. But you see how it has all come together?"

I did not. "I understand who our killer is, but I confess I am still confused as to how exactly he enacted the plan. There is still the matter of his alibi."

Holmes eyed me for a disconcertingly long moment, the twinkle dimming a bit. He shrugged. "Well, if one of us knows, that is sufficient," he stated.

He jotted down a missive and sent Billy off to Scotland Yard. "Tomorrow," he declared, "all will be clear, and our Mr. Oswald will be uncomfortable in a cell where he belongs."

In the light of day, Mrs. Oswald's drawing room looked larger, the air drifting in from the tall French windows. That same calico cat lay upon the divan, stretched out on her back as if she did not have a care in the world. She was deep asleep.

Mrs. Oswald was already standing, and, once again, she took both our hands in turn, pressing gently and welcoming us to sit.

She fixed the folds of her skirt as she took her seat. "I've not been able to rest since your last visit, Mr. Holmes. Why were you asking about my husband's whereabouts?"

Holmes leaned forward from where he sat next to the entirely unbothered cat. He clasped his hands together. "I'm afraid, madam, that by bringing me your husband's private letters – and you must be aware of this – you have necessitated an investigation into what secret a blackmailer may be able to hold over your husband's head?"

She fiddled nervously with the button of her waistshirt. "I was aware of that, yes."

"And you are aware that this information may be dire?" he stared carefully into her face, as if trying to impress upon her the seriousness of her actions.

She inhaled deeply, steadying herself. "I've long suspected my husband may be tempted to act in self-interest instead of the best interest of his country. I likely will not be shocked by any facts that come to light. As to what effect they may have upon my own situation, I suppose I will have to deal with that as it unfolds."

Holmes looked disconcerted with this declaration. He gazed intently and, to my surprise, sadly at her. "That is an admirable attitude, madam. I'm sure it will help as you find yourself faced with sudden, unexpected changes."

She paled a bit at his ominous warning and nodded mutely, gazing intently back at him.

Holmes broke the contact and stood, taking a circle around the room and petting the calico gently as he passed.

"This may be an odd question, but does your husband have an unusual clock? Likely recently purchased?" he asked.

She looked caught off-kilter by the bewildering question. "As a matter of fact, he brought home a strange looking thing that he found somewhere. We don't use it, though. It's more a bric-a-brac type oddity that caught his fancy."

"Could I trouble you to fetch it for me?"

She came back in with an exact copy of the strange skeleton alarm clock I had seen in Miss White's flat. Holmes looked simultaneously pleased and dismayed to see it. He took it from her gently.

"When did he purchase this?"

"A little over a week ago."

Holmes took a deep breath and set it on the mantelpiece, fiddling with the knobs.

"What does this have to do with my husband's letters, sir?" Mrs. Oswald questioned, her voice curious.

"That may be proven in a moment, madam." He stepped back, and we waited for whatever he expected to happen. He had evidently set the alarm for only a few seconds; the little bell went off, sending the skeleton into a jittery little happy dance.

A woman's clear voice rang out, operatic, startling me and Mrs. Oswald. The woman spun around, hand to her chest, searching for someone hiding in the room. My hand had tightened around my walking stick, as well.

"There is no one else here," Holmes assured softly. He went to the bird cage and shifted the cover off. "Little Bella is serenading us." The bird fell quiet, bobbing happily up and down. Holmes put a lithe finger through the bars, and the creature put its paw there.

"I'm confused," Mrs. Oswald confessed haltingly after a long period of prolonged silence.

"Understandably," Holmes reassured. "Tell me, is this cage always in this room?"

Still looking perplexed, our hostess shook her head. "At times, my husband brings her into his chamber. She also visits a specialized veterinarian on a regular basis."

"Of course, so you would not miss her if she were gone for a little while," Holmes murmured. I could sense that familiar excitement in his voice when he stumbled upon the key to a puzzle, tempered only by his consideration for Mrs. Oswald's feelings. Even being as slow-witted as I was, the chain of events were clear to me, and I realized what was to come to light would upheave this woman's life.

"I will do you the courtesy of warning you that Inspector Lestrade from Scotland Yard will be paying your husband a visit this afternoon. He will place your husband under arrest."

He would tell her no more, reassuring her that the police would likely prefer to speak to her. He pressed a soothing hand to her arm when she seemed inclined to press him for an explanation.

"You have proven yourself an admirably practical woman, madam. This quality will serve you well through what is to come."

Lestrade was happy to see us, eager to hear Holmes relay the events that had led to the man's arrest. Mr. Oswald was currently locked in a holding cell.

"Well, I can't say I'm surprised, Mr. Holmes. You prance in here, seemingly pick an unsolved murder at random, and supply me with a culprit all neat and tidy wrapped in a nice little bow in just a few days. And with a prominent figure at the centre as well." There was grudging respect in the inspector's tone, tinged with not an inconsiderable amount of resentment.

"People usually appreciate gifts wrapped in nice little bows, Lestrade," Holmes countered good-naturedly. "And to be fair, I had the benefit of Mrs. Oswald visiting me and setting me on the leads that cleared the matter up."

"Unusually gracious of you, Holmes. Now, can you please explain to me what is going on?"

"Simple. Watson?"

"Um," I stuttered, put on the spot. "Well, it seems to me that the parrot is the key to it." I glanced at Holmes, who nodded encouragingly. I continued, "The next door neighbor heard Miss White singing, but what she heard was the parrot. Mr. Oswald, as Miss White's former paramour, had a key to her flat. He entered while she was cooking dinner around five, strangled her, and then," here I looked to Holmes once more, unsure, "to avoid anyone seeing, went to the alley and slid the birdcage into the room through the broken window."

Holmes nodded and picked up the story, "This provided him with the perfect alibi because he, after turning off the stove to avoid a fire, went to dinner and the opera with his wife. He returned in the early hours of the morning, slunk into the alley and removed the cage."

Lestrade looked befuddled. "But how would he have guessed the bird would sing when he needed it to?"

"Easy. He trained her. Parrots are highly intelligent birds. It does not take long to teach them new mimicry."

"The clock," I explained patiently at Lestrade's annoyed look. "Mr. Oswald has the exact same clock in his room, and we tested it as a cue on the bird earlier today."

Lestrade let out an amazed chuckle. "It's no wonder, Holmes, that you often appear to one-up me. The sheer ridiculousness and audacity of some of these criminals."

"Very creative," Holmes agreed, skimming over the insult.

"This all might be a bit hard to prove."

Holmes shrugged. "You have the bird, the clock, I suspect a key to Miss White's flat somewhere amongst the man's effects, and a witness by the name of Michael Everett who can supply you with the connection between Miss

White and Mr. Oswald, as well as the catalyst for this crime."

We were interrupted by a knock on the door. A young constable poked his head in.

"A Mrs. Oswald is here, inspector. She is adamant about speaking to you."

We met her in the hall. She had changed into an immaculate walking dress and hat. She looked at us with clear, steady eyes.

She waved away Lestrade's invitation to enter his office. "Inspector Gregson has already given me a general sketch of events. May I see my husband for a moment?"

Lestrade looked annoyed at Gregson and unsure about the request. He cast a glance at Holmes as if for guidance. "That is quite unorthodox, ma'am," he hedged.

"I only wish to ask him a question or two. I need the truth from his own mouth. One cannot function in an ethical or moral way without truth."

Holmes looked at her appreciatively. "On the whole, I'm of the same mind."

"Perhaps I should have wed you."

Lestrade and I felt the understandable sharp awkwardness of such a bold statement, but Holmes chuckled softly, unbothered.

She grew sober and tugged gently on the fingertips of her lace gloves. "Well, inspector? May I have just a minute of time with my husband alone?"

"A minute, but not alone."

We escorted her into the dingy holding cell. She looked entirely out of place there, bedecked in her immaculate sage-green dress and expensive hat.

Mr. Oswald looked surprised to see his wife. The surprise melted into a flush of shame as she placidly circled the old wooden table and stood at his side.

"The inspectors here tell me that you are responsible for the death of that young opera singer," she stated dully.

"It was a misunder-"

He did not get through his sentence. Pure rage flashed across the woman's face and, quicker than could be seen, she pulled her hat pin from her hair and flung herself at him, aiming for his neck.

The glint of the sharp item froze me, but Holmes reacted with lightning quick reflexes, nearly vaulting over the table and scattering the chairs in his effort to reach her before she could deal a killing blow. He tackled her bodily, landing in a heap of struggling limbs. She continued to fight, spitting invectives at her husband and giving Holmes plenty of trouble keeping her under control.

"You murdered that girl!" she cried, her voice cracking, "You strangled her and sat next to me at the opera as if she were nothing!"

Mr. Oswald, from behind the shield of Lestrade's body, unwisely kept speaking. "I could not lose you!"

That did not help. His wife screamed again, lurching from Holmes's grasp for a moment. She made it to the table before he secured her once again. Far beyond being gentlemanly, he picked her up and swung her out of the room, manhandling her into Lestrade's office.

The commotion had caused a crowd of officers in the hallway, but the inspector barked at them at all to mind their own business and secured the cell door before following us.

Holmes was leaning over the woman as she sat, breathing heavily in the inspector's chair. She was still flushed with rage and defiantly refused to meet his gaze, but she was sitting obediently, and I could see his softly whispered words were having a calming effect.

"You mustn't let your anger ruin your future, madam," he urged, "You are an innocent in this, but murder, not matter how you may justify it, will not allow you to walk away from this without consequence." He took her by the shoulders firmly, forcing her to look at him. "He is not worth it."

"That girl-" she began, voice trembling with emotion.

"Was as innocent as you are. We know. But the gallows wait for him. Do not rush justice only to your own harm."

She pressed her fingers to her eyes for a long time before glancing up at Lestrade. "Forgive me, gentlemen, for my unforgivable behavior. If you must arrest me, sir, could I please ask that you do so discreetly?"

Holmes rose. "Arrest you for what?" he asked with feigned confusion.

He glanced at Lestrade. "I saw nothing occur worthy of arrest, did you?"

Lestrade glared but shook his head. "I suppose I didn't see anything. I had turned around to close the cell, you see," he lied.

Glancing at me for confirmation, which I gave without hesitation, Holmes gestured to the office door. "Seeing as no crime has been committed, you are free to go."

She looked startled but quickly obeyed, apologizing once again in a low murmur before leaving. We followed her out, watching her go.

Holmes let out a small chuckle. "An admirable woman, indeed."

I frowned curiously at him. "Strange. I would have thought her emotional outburst would have diminished her in your estimation."

He laughed again. "Not at all. Had I been in her place, I cannot say I would have acted any differently. At times, emotional outbursts are the most expected – even logical – course of action."

He bid Lestrade adieu, and we settled into the relative warmth of the hansom cab. The sun was just beginning its descent, and our time spent at Scotland Yard would result in us missing a very important caller who would grace us with an ordinary walking stick and a fantastic story.

Holmes leaned back, still chuckling. "One small silver lining – Mrs. Oswald is now a free woman."

"Are you seriously considering her suggestion?" I teased. "Serving as her second husband?"

He laughed. "Marrying a younger, smarter man who does not chase skirts behind her back would be a definite upgrade," he said, the arrogance of the statement negated by the sparkle of mischief in his eyes. "But alas, you know my domestic preferences, and marriage does not align with my need for solitude." While Holmes was indeed not a man easily swayed by feminine qualities, he did seem to have an admirable view of Mrs. Oswald, or even a protective view, going so far as to send me to Baskerville Hall without him in order to testify in Oswald's trial and do what he could to spare the wife a scandal larger than that which was already inevitable (one of the most revered names in England, indeed!)

"Speaking of marriage," I started, realizing he was in a good mood and had been free from his chemical distractions for at least three days, "There is a small matter I've been meaning to broach with you."

"Indeed?"

"You may feel free to refuse; you have no obligation to spare my feelings," I blustered on, feeling suddenly nervous as he stared impassively at me across the way. "But I was wondering if you would mind serving as best man at my wedding? There is very little required of you, a passing of the rings, and the ceremony will be short-"

"Watson," he cut me off curtly. Then he smiled. "I was beginning to think you'd never ask."

It was the winter season in London, 1898, when Holmes and I encountered the strange case of the Stanhope orphan and her untimely death. Holmes had been unoccupied for a few days; besides a few trivial cases here and there over the last month, his last engaging problem had been the tragedy of the strange dancing men. I could detect a strain of self-recrimination in my dear friend's attitude towards the outcome of the whole matter, as if the loss of his client and the near death of Elsie Cubitt had been entirely his fault. No amount of reasoning could convince Holmes that his delay in deciphering that damned code did not make him responsible for the violence that followed. Any time I broached the sensitive topic, he waved me off with a dismissive hand as if the matter did not perturb him in the least, but I knew him too well to be fooled by his act. The weather did little to alleviate the morose atmosphere of our rooms, and Holmes, freed for some time from the clutches and "cure" of his seven percent solution, fell into a worrisome ennui that found him lounging in his chair throughout the day in his mouse-colored dressing gown.

This was how we found ourselves on a dreary morning before breakfast when a bustle at the front signaled the arrival of a disturbed guest. We heard Mrs. Hudson's exasperated protests as someone hurriedly stomped up the 17 steps to our rooms and burst in with in a harried and urgent whirlwind. He was a man of about five and thirty, who had evidently dressed in a hurry; his expensive suit was creased and a button on his waistcoat had been overlooked. He bore the tell-tale black armband that signified a period of grief. He rushed into the room, ignoring our dear landlady as she tried to stop him.

His dark hair flopped excitedly over his forehead as he bounced on his heels anxiously.

"Mr. Holmes, I presume?" he asked desperately, somehow instinctively honing in on my friend in his place by the roaring fire.

Holmes's eyes, for the first time in weeks, twinkled with amusement. With a silent jerk of his chin, he acknowledged the man's words and sent an irritated Mrs. Hudson back down the stairs.

"I apologize for my behavior," the man began, speaking so fast he was nearly stumbling over his words, "but in just a moment, my wife will be here and you must humour her, sir. She is unwell. I could not convince her-"

He broke off at the sound of the front door once again being opened by Mrs. Hudson then urgently whispered, "I left her to pay the driver." He dove for the door, smiling at the dark figure stepping onto the landing. "Darling! Forgive me for rushing ahead!"

The woman who glided in was wrapped head to toe in mourning dress and veil. I could see not one inch of her skin or features besides the slight curl of dark hair pinned beneath her ears. It was clear the couple was suffering some loss.

Holmes and I stood at her strange entrance. She did not respond to her husband, but dipped delicately in greeting. I arranged the chairs to allow her a comfortable seat, but she moved the basket chair until her back was to the window, the weak rays of the rising sun obscuring her form even more. She folded her hands over her lap, the slight tilt of her veil the only indication she was alive.

Her husband sat next to her, his manner nervous. He cleared his throat. "Mr. Holmes, you may know my wife from her maiden name, Miss Stanhope, of the Stanhope tragedy."

Holmes tilted his head, his interest piqued. "I am," he affirmed carefully, his voice soft. "But I am also familiar with your recent marriage and ... current troubles. My condolences, Mrs. Brackenreid. I cannot imagine suffering a loss as you have."

It took me a moment to search my mind for why the Stanhope name was familiar, but then I remembered the story of the Stanhope orphan, the only child to survive a devastating train accident in 1873. Her entire family had perished, leaving her a substantial fortune and a fame that had forced her into a hermit lifestyle in the confines of her manor. In a surprising turn, she had emerged from her hideaway in the previous year to marry a barrister beneath her station, and then suffered the loss of their newborn four weeks ago. Her mourning veil suddenly took on new meaning to me and, stung with a sudden flush of sympathy, I expressed my sincere condolences.

"It is one thing on the heels of another," she finally spoke. Her voice was pitched low, barely a whisper. It forced me and Holmes to lean forward to hear her. She did not seem to notice our struggle and continued, her tone wavering with emotion, "There is a vast conspiracy against me, Mr. Holmes. You must help."

Holmes, still leaning forward with his elbows on the armrests of his chair, frowned in interested confusion. "Can you elaborate?"

Her husband, Mr. Brackenreid, cut in, "My wife believes that her parents' death-"

Holmes held up a halting hand. "If you don't mind, I'd prefer to hear your wife's worries from her own mouth."

That seemed to draw our guests up short. A tense silence settled for a moment as the couple glanced at each other. Mr. Brackenreid finally nodded his assent at his wife and she began, her voice never rising above that hoarse whisper. I wonder if it was due to weeping. "Mr. Holmes, my entire life, I have been dogged by insidious forces that murdered my parents and have now murdered my young child." Here, she gave way to a burst of choked crying. Her hand disappeared under her veil to brush at her eyes. Holmes reached into the loose pocket of his dressing gown and retrieved a handkerchief, passing it to her. He leaned forward to press it into her hand, peering intently through the veil with a deep sympathy.

She dabbed at her tears and then took a deep breath.

In the moment of silence, Holmes took his own deep breath and, obviously choosing his words very carefully, said gently, "Mrs. Brackenreid, forgive my directness, but your parents were killed in a railway accident. A tragic accident, no doubt, but hardly an assassination."

"That's the brilliance of it, Mr. Holmes."

I could see a sliver of irritation slipping through Holmes's mask despite how sympathetic I knew he was to the woman's loss. "And why, pray tell, would these assassins derail an entire train, killing numerous people, to target your parents?"

"They wished to switch me, like a changeling, with a child from their world."

Holmes cut a quick glance in my direction. "Their world?"

"Have you heard of the Hollow Earth Society, sirs?"

I leaned back in my chair, fighting a flood of worry for this woman's mental well-being. Her husband looked down and away, clearly ill at ease with his wife's behavior. He shifted uncomfortably in his seat, the legs creaking beneath him.

Holmes too seemed to be holding back some stronger response, flexing his fingers and biting the inside of his lip. After a moment, he nodded. "I have."

"The ones who live there, the precursors to mankind as we know it, wished to snatch me away, but they could not find me in the train that day."

Holmes brought his steepled fingers up to press against the bridge of his nose and then rested them under his chin. "And your child?"

"Having failed at retrieving me, they clearly set their sights on my son."

"But there was no changeling."

"There was!" At last, her voice rose, a stridency in her tone that was startling. "Do you imagine that thing was my boy? No, my boy is somewhere with them."

Mr. Brackenreid closed his eyes in dismay. His worry and sorrow was palpable. Holmes, for all his calculated practicality, was no stranger to compassion, and I glanced at him to see his own expression darken with sympathy and worry. He laced his fingers together and stared downwards to the smoldering fire behind the grate for a long while as the clock loudly ticked the seconds by in the tense silence.

Finally, he spoke with undisguised concern. He directed his words to Mr. Brackenreid instead of his wife. "Sir, I do not mean to be insensitive, but I believe your wife would fare better seeking the services of an alienist or a specialized medical doctor-"

Mrs. Brackenreid, née Stanhope, made a choking noise of despair and stood, nearly knocking over the chair. "I did not come here to be insulted," she spat and then noisily bustled her way past her husband.

Holmes half stood, a protest and apology uncharacteristically stuttering on his tongue. I too began to stand, ready to forestall her departure; the woman clearly needed help, even it if was not the help she believed she needed. She was too determined to be free of our company, however, and we could not prevent her from stomping her way back down the stairs. Mr. Brackenreid had risen as well, though he fought little to keep his wife in the room. He gave us a rueful look, apologizing for bothering us.

He glanced out of the window at the lightening sky and sighed. "I appreciate that you made an attempt to listen, Mr. Holmes."

"I did not mean to slight your wife," the detective said, looking discomfited.

"You did not. There is really no way to counteract her claims without drawing attention to her delusions."

"You may seriously consider finding her appropriate care," I cut in. "I know some private doctors who are adept at discretion."

Brackenreid nodded but still looked unsure. "Sound advice, doctor. I musn't leave her on the pavement for too long, especially while it is still relatively dark outside. Good morning, gentlemen. Again, my deepest thanks."

With that, they were gone as strangely as they had appeared.

I glanced at Holmes. He looked unsettled, frowning in the direction of the closed door.

"Poor girl," I murmured.

Holmes grunted in agreement, and then took the few steps to his bookshelf, took down his messy commonplace book, and then sunk down in his seat. I knew what that meant and left him to it, helping Mrs. Hudson as she brought up our tray of breakfast.

I was only half-way through my first cup of tea when he shut the book with a decided thump and sighed.

"Discover anything of interest?" I asked.

He shook his head and strummed his fingers on the worn cover. "Very little after the train accident. Her money was held by a lawyer until she was of age. She rarely leaves her home or engages in public life. She is a collector of antiquities, specifically rare books. Last year, unexpectedly, she wed Mr.

Jeremy Brackenreid, a new barrister, and in September of this year, she gave birth to a son. The infant sadly died weeks ago, suddenly, in his crib."

"Loss of that magnitude can manifest in irrational behavior." I did not mention that I spoke from personal experience, having lost my wife and newborn six years ago, but Holmes's gaze flickered to me, evidently reading my thoughts. As usual, he did not address it head on, but hummed sympathetically.

"Indeed. A sad progression but hopefully not the end of her story. There must be some light in all that tragedy."

It was a strangely sentimental thing for Holmes to say, and I could not help but wonder if it was directed towards me. I cleared my throat and gestured to the delicious fried potatoes and hardboiled eggs that our admirable landlady had prepared for us, but before Holmes could join me (or, more likely, rebuff my invitation), the door swung open once again, causing a gust of wind and upsetting some of my papers.

Mr. Brackenreid flew into the room, eyes wild with panic. "Good God!" he exclaimed, his face white with shock, "She's done it! I did not think her capable, but she has done it!"

Holmes stood, all attention. "Take a breath, man," he barked. "What has she done?"

The man reeled as if about to pass out. I tensed, ready to go to his aid, but he rallied at the last moment, managing to stay upright. "She asked me to step into the Eason and Son bookstore and enquire as to whether they had any information on Geneva bibles," he began, voice wavering. "But in my absence, she went to the roof and threw herself off!"

Holmes started, looking thunderstruck by the news. "Where is she?"

"Someone has fetched an ambulance. I know no one else in the area-"

I pushed forward, "Lead me to her!" I demanded, ushering the man down the stairs. Holmes spared a second to fling off his dressing gown and followed at my heels in only his shirtsleeves and waistcoat.

Eason and Son was on a side street the branched off a few blocks north from Baker Street. It was a quiet area, and even now with the tragedy at hand, there were only a handful of bystanders watching as the body was loaded into the back of the ambulance. I could gather from the lack of urgency that the woman was dead. Holmes, I could tell, had come to the same conclusion, his footsteps slowing against the wet cobblestone as we circled a shocked fruit vendor with his cart. By the time we were close enough to view the body, the driver was already closing the doors and readying his horse. Mr. Brackenreid darted forward, declaring his relation to the patient, and was allowed to swing himself upwards into the carriage next to his lifeless wife.

Holmes craned his neck, analyzing the content of the cart and attempting to move forward, but his way was barred. "I'd like to view the body," he snapped impatiently.

The driver was unaffected by his tone and merely shook his head. "Have some respect, sir. You can speak to the coroner if you want approval to examine her."

The horse snuffled and Holmes watched with irritation as its hooves clomped down the street. The lollygaggers didn't seem to know what to do, standing about and murmuring in hushed but excited undertones. Holmes bent down and looked at the wet pavement where the body had landed, frowning.

"What are you searching for?" I asked soberly, leaning down at his side.

He shook his head. "No blood, but the amount of force that needs to be exerted on a person's head to lead to fatality does not always result in loss of blood."

I hummed in agreement. He stood and glanced upwards at the top of the bookstore. It was a good sized double story with the proprietors' living quarters at the top.

"Doctor, in your medical opinion, do you believe a fall from that height could lead to death?" Holmes asked me.

I nodded. "It's not a given but a possibility. A brain injury could result in instantaneous death if she landed right … or wrong, more accurately."

Holmes grunted. It seemed inarguable that this was a clear case of suicide, but Holmes paced the pavement intently for a prolonged length of time. What he was looking for, only heaven knows, but he evidently did not find it, breathing out an impatient huff and rubbing a hand across his wide brow as the idle bystanders continued to murmur and loiter around the empty scene.

"Watson, make a round and ask those vendors on the other side of the street what they saw." He turned and approached a girl who had evidently been halfway through setting up a small flower stand on the corner. I obeyed, crossing the street and nodded somberly to the costermongers looking dismayed but strangely thrilled at such a dramatic interruption to their morning business.

"Morning," I nodded, "I'll leave off the customary descriptor as, indeed, the day has not begun in any way that could be described as 'good'. May I ask you what you witnessed?"

"Is that Sherlock Holmes?" one of the women asked instead, an excited gleam in her eye as she watched my friend across the way.

I coughed delicately, used to this sort of reaction. "Indeed," I answered smoothly, "and he would be eternally grateful" – as if Holmes would ever be so to anyone – "if you could provide us with the details of what you saw of this poor girl's death."

The lady nearly vibrated with the very idea of Sherlock Holmes being eternally grateful to her and told me that she had been loading the cart with her daily supply of apples when she had heard Mr. Brackenreid call out. She first looked to him, standing on the kerb with his arms flown outwards, staring up at the sky. She then looked up as well to see what he was gawking at when the deceased flung herself down to the ground.

"Face-first?" I asked.

"Yes," she nodded, "arms outwards like wings."

"You're sure of it?"

She nodded, a look of irritation crossing her face. I glanced at the other vendors who had gathered about me. "And is that what all of you saw as well?" These nods were more hesitant and therefore worrisome. I politely thanked them for their time and met Holmes, who had finished up his interrogation of the flower seller efficiently and was waiting for me in the middle of the street. He was frowning, that look of abstract frustration on his face that I was familiar with.

"Is something the matter, Holmes?" I asked.

"The young lady tells me she witnessed Miss Stanhope fling herself from the roof after her husband called out in surprise," he answered distractedly.

"That is what my witnesses claim as well. One noticed that the woman had her arms spread outwards," I told him, aware that any small detail may prove important to Holmes.

He cut me a quick frown. "Are you sure that's what she said? That's odd. My flower girl there says her hands were at her chest."

"Perhaps if they looked up at different times, they may both be right. The first image, pressed into the mind by shock, may be the image that sticks. The flower girl looked up while her arms were down; the fruit seller looked up a second later, once the woman had raised her arms," I theorized, feeling proud of myself.

But Holmes shook his head like I was a bee buzzing about his ear, and I felt myself flush with irritation and a bit of embarrassment.

Of course – and thankfully – he did not notice. "Something is amiss," he murmured, "however, it's quite unlike me that I cannot pinpoint exactly what it is."

"Perhaps it is simply the tragedy of such an end for a young woman who had experienced so much undeserved sorrow in her life," I suggested.

Surprisingly, Holmes nodded in agreement. After a few more seconds watching him stand, surveying the scene with those sharp grey eyes darting here and there, cataloging, I followed his lead as he began the trek back to our warm rooms.

It seemed odd to return to the placid, comforting quiet of Baker Street. It felt as if the last twenty minutes or so had been a strange waking nightmare. Holmes retook his seat next to the smoldering embers of our fire and stared off into the distance. I resumed my meal in a numb state, hardly tasting anything but at a loss as to what else to do.

The next morning, Holmes knocked me up around six o'clock, looking impatient as I groped around for my watch, bleary-eyed and confused.

"I assure you, it is morning, doctor, though perhaps a smidge earlier than you're accustomed to," he informed me dryly. I confirmed by squinting irritably at my timepiece in the gloom of the barely emerging sun struggling to break through the winter fog.

"What has possessed you to wake me at this hour?" I snapped. My sleep had been fitful, plagued by recurring visions of the misfortune I had witnessed the previous day. Poor Mrs. Brackenreid had needed help, and there was no small part of me that felt we had handled her complaint poorly. I wondered if Holmes felt the same way, and this thought caused my annoyance at him to soften.

"I am determined to visit the morgue and make a closer examination of Miss Stanhope's body," he told me as I swung my legs out of the bed.

I peered up at him, confused but interested. "To what point, Holmes?"

"For my own peace of mind, Watson," he confessed. "Would you like to accompany me?"

It was an unnecessary question, and I rose quickly to change as he fetched a cab.

We were on our way in no time, and as we rattled down the cobblestone streets, I asked, "Have you come to any clarity on what was bothering you yesterday about her death?"

He shook his head. "No, except that the feeling will not go away."

"Was it something regarding the body?"

"I hardly saw the body. And thus our little day trip to the jewel of London."

"Jewel" was drawled with that dry sarcasm Holmes was so adept at. Indeed, the mortuaries of England were not a point of pride. The lack of sanitation and space always made me shudder. The St. Pancras Coroner's Court was the best of a bad lot, having been built as a direct answer to the unhygienic state of other morgues and the concern that was expressed over the delicate work of post-mortems being completed in such places, but the smell that wafted from it was still enough to fell the sturdiest of men. As a doctor, I was accustomed to it, and Holmes had long ago proven himself inhumanly impervious to unpleasant smells, sights, and sounds (at least, while on a case), but that did not make the trip any less odious.

"I admit, a morgue is not the most pleasant place to spend one's time," I commented dryly.

In the early morning sunlight, the red brick of the gothic-inspired building glistened with dew, and the morgue was quiet. Unlike the cramped shed of Kew, this morgue allowed us plenty of room; a fit made even more comfortable by the fact that there was no body waiting for us even though we had sent word ahead.

The coroner, a man of about thirty with birdlike features and a wide smile named Miller, shook our hands and, to his credit, did not react to Holmes's brusque manner of immediately demanding to know where the body was.

"I wanted to take a look at Mrs. Brackenreid. She committed suicide yesterday morning."

"Yes, the woman who jumped from a roof? Well, that may be a wee bit tricky, detective. She is buried."

Holmes raised his eyebrows in disbelief. "She is buried? It's not even seven in the morning, sir."

The coroner shrugged. "Her husband was adamant she be buried as soon as possible."

"Did you conduct a post-mortem?"

"I was allowed a cursory look over the body. I noted a deep contusion on the back of her head that indicated a fall from a great height. There were also injuries on her back and shoulders that indicated that she landed flat on her back."

"So it seems there was no last minute decision to save herself?"

"A fall from that height may not have afforded her the time to have second thoughts. It's a quick fall, thankfully."

"Did you notice anything else about the body that was of special note?"

"As I said, the exam was … cursory."

Holmes pressed his fingers to the bridge of his nose. "Rigor mortis?"

"I did not arrive until late in the evening so rigor mortis was already well under way. She was stiff and cold, so time of death becomes hard to pin down. The best I could estimate is that she had died 8 to 16 hours before."

"And what exact time did you arrive?"

"Approximately seven o'clock. There seemed to be no haste since there was no indication of foul play."

Holmes cut me a side glance, a flush of irritation on his face. "No haste to examine her but all haste to bury her?" he interrogated, voice strident.

For the first time, Miller looked defensive. "I thought it odd myself, sir. To be clear, I did not dally in arriving; I was not called in a timely manner."

Holmes evidently realized his impatience was misplaced, and his expression softened. "Are her effects still here?" he asked, gentling his tone. It was the closest he'd come to an apology.

The man seemed to understand. He nodded with a flicker of a polite smile. "Yes, let me retrieve her box."

He left briefly to a connected alcove and returned with a wood box. Holmes poked around at the contents. Inside was the emptied purse of the deceased and the items that she had carried in it: lip rouge, a mirror, calling cards, and a small, stubbed pencil. Holmes stared at the contents for a long while, quietly absorbed.

Finally, he shook his head and lightly pushed the box away with his finger.

He strode out of the morgue without a goodbye, forehead creased in consternation.

I bid Miller good day and thanked him for his help, rushing to catch up with the detective. "Holmes," I called out, trying to regulate my breathing as I finally reached him as he was stepping off the kerb and casting his gaze about for a hansom cab.

He didn't speak until we had alighted into a four-wheeler; he directed the driver to Victoria Station, and I frowned at him in confusion. "Holmes, why are we going to the train station?"

"I'm sorry, old man," he apologized even though he did not sound particularly apologetic, "I suppose I shouldn't presume upon your time. I am going to Kent to visit the widower. I'd be forever grateful if you'd join me."

I snorted, remembering my words to the fruit seller the morning before. Holmes looked a bit taken aback by my mirth, and I rushed to assure him that

I was not slighting him. "As always, it would be my pleasure to join you, though I do wonder what you hope to accomplish."

"Whatever do you mean, Watson?" he grumbled impatiently, "Where would you have me go, if not to the house of the deceased?"

As usual, he had a point. I redirected the conversation to the heart of the matter. "Do you believe she committed suicide, Holmes, or do you believe this is a criminal investigation?"

"Well, if we want to be very technical in regards the law, suicide would be a criminal act."

"But you would only be interested in such a crime if the context was unclear," I pressed. "Therefore, do you believe she committed suicide but the context is unclear, or do you believe she did not commit suicide?"

I saw a rare look of uncertainty cross his face. Finally, he admitted, "I hesitate to believe anything without any evidence pointing me in any direction."

"So you hope to find some evidence in Kent?"

"Evidence or simply peace of mind." Again, that uncertainty made its way to the surface. "I admit that I must face the fact that if she did indeed commit suicide with no mitigating factors worthy of note, that means that my unkindness perhaps contributed to her state of mind." It was a strange thing for Holmes to confess, even if it wasn't a strange thing for him to feel. I understood, however, because I too regretted my abruptness with the woman when she visited our rooms. I knew that the feeling was unfounded, though.

"Your behavior towards her, Holmes, was not unkind," I reassured him. "At least, no less unkind than my own behavior. So if feel you must bear the brunt of guilt, I must bear it with you."

He arched an eyebrow at that and fell silent, staring out at the early morning bustle of Cromwell Road. He was no more talkative on the train, turning inwards in that peculiar way that I had come to learn meant he was deep in thought, turning over details to discover connective tissue to aid his deductions. I knew it was not going well by the slight crease in his brow and the way he rubbed absently at his right palm with the thumb of his other hand. It was a recipe for unpleasantness, so I knew it was best not to disturb him. I picked up the morning edition of *The Times* that I had procured at the station and read the small obituary for Mrs. Brackenreid. It contained no information beyond what we already knew and was painfully short and to the point. I suppose her husband felt it best to be brief considering the details of her death and state of mind. I wanted to mention it to Holmes, but folded the section over and saved it for when he would be more receptive to what was likely a triviality.

It was only when we had stopped and disembarked, making our way through the small crowd at the station that I ventured to pass him the paper. He scanned it quickly and then flicked it into a trash receptacle near the door to the ticket room. "A very anti-climactic summary of a tragic life," he murmured.

"She was a recluse, Holmes. Not much was known about her," I countered.

"I would assume her husband knew much about her," he countered back.

"Perhaps it was done from respect. Knowing her preference for privacy."

He hummed thoughtfully and then conceded, "Perhaps."

He procured a hansom cab to bring us to the Brackenreid house, an old estate that had belonged to the Stanhope family before their untimely end and passed on to their orphaned daughter. The house was 18th century, built in an elegant neo-classical style with a beautiful garden of trees and rosebushes that lined the dirt drive, nearly brushing the sides of the hansom cab as we rattled our way up to the front door.

Holmes spared the beauty very little consideration, bounding from the cab and knocking brusquely on the front door. The footman announced our visit and led us into a small sunroom through a set of French doors. A long-haired fluffy cat was stretched out on the divan, bathing in the weak winter sunlight. A few decorative palm trees dotted the perimeter. Mr. Brackenreid was striding towards us as we entered, his hand held out to shake ours. His hands trembled noticeably, and the redness of his eyes spoke of his private expressions of grief.

We greeted him, apologizing for calling without sending word.

Holmes nodded somberly at him as we took the seats our host gestured us towards. "My condolences, sir, once more."

Brackenreid began to speak, but the hoarseness of his voice forced him to clear his throat before he could continue. We did him the gentlemanly courtesy of pretending not to notice. "I'm grateful for them," he told us, a waver to his words that made me feel a surge of sympathy. "I must admit I'm surprised to receive you as visitors. Forgive me, but I was under the impression that suicides were entirely too mundane to catch the investigative interest of Sherlock Holmes."

Holmes was quiet for a moment; when he did speak, his face was his usual mask of neutral pragmatism, but his voice was gentle and sincere. "Despite what the press may say, I am not an automaton or calculating machine." He cast a quick, affectionately accusatory glance in my direction. "Your wife's death has weighed on me."

Brackenreid frowned, looking strangely displeased. I gathered the idea of such a personal loss being of detached professional interest to the detective made him bristle. It was an understandable reaction. "Thus you felt compelled to pursue it?"

"I never said I was pursuing anything. I am curious as to what the post-mortem may have told you about why she behaved the way she did."

"We learned very little." A slight hesitation. "But I have a theory."

A spark of interest flared in my friend's eye. "Indeed? I'm curious."

"Expressing theories to the 'great detective' is understandably daunting. I feel as if I'm being tested."

"I'm merely curious. You lived with her. Your observations will likely be informative."

We sat in silence for so long that I started to feel uncomfortable. Holmes, by nature an impatient man, could still wait out a client's hesitation for as long as necessary. At last, Brackenreid seemed to come to some decision and stood with a sigh. He wiped gently at his eyes.

"Come," he beckoned. We followed him through the portrait-lined halls and entered a heavy set of double doors. This room was darker, with heavy curtains blocking the light of the windows. It was large, and each wall was covered by nearly ceiling high bookshelves filled with books.

"My wife was a collector, as I said before," Brackenreid commented, bidding us entry. He opened one of the curtains to let in some light. "This is her library. Sunlight can damage the items, so it's often dark in here." He guided Holmes over to darker corner of, what seemed to be, older volumes. He gently pulled down a small pocket-sized book of Marlowe's plays and handed it carefully to Holmes. "You see here; the green and yellow pigment on many of these book covers are chipping."

Holmes turned the thing over in his hands, falling into a contemplative silence. Then, he nodded. "And thus possibly toxic."

"I'm afraid I'm at a loss, Holmes," I interrupted. I knew nothing of collected books, so I was struggling to see the connection.

The detective handed the item back to its new owner. "Many of these books' pigments contain arsenic and lead," he explained. "Pigment, unlike dye, chips and releases the toxin. If she handled these books regularly, she may have been slowly poisoning herself. Poisons also can-"

Everything fell into place. "Also can have an effect on mental faculties, yes, I know."

Brackenreid made an expansive gesture to encompass the wall of shelves. "As you can see, gentlemen, she has many of these books."

Holmes perused the collection for a few moments, that peculiar abstracted look on his face that told me that his mind was deep at work. His attention was caught by the opposite corner of the room where a small armchair sat next to a table. On the table was a beautiful leather-bound edition of the King James Bible and a small pot of oil. Holmes ran his hand over the cover. "This book does not seem to be an antique."

Brackenreid shook his head. "No, but it held great sentimental value to her. That was her father's bible. My wife never professed to any zealous religious beliefs, but she treasured that book."

"Indeed. It appears she took very good care of it. Is this neatsfoot oil she used to care for the leather?"

"Yes, quite regularly. She became almost obsessive after the death of our son."

Holmes hummed under his breath, then rubbed the tips of his fingers together, casting an obvious look of worry towards the shelf of old books he had touched. "May I use your washroom?"

"Of course. Upstairs, to the left. I can have Williams-"

"No need," Holmes brushed off quickly. I knew him well enough to know that his worry about touching the pigments had been an act, and his disinclination to have the footman escort him around the house indicated that he planned to do some snooping.

It was now my job to act natural. I followed Holmes's example and took a slow walk around the room, perusing, but not touching, the books on display. The late Mrs. Brackenreid had indeed been an avid collector, and I noticed some very old volumes, particularly of old folklore and fairytales. I wondered how much all of this could fetch on the market, but felt too insensitive to ask such a question at this time.

Instead, I inquired, "What will you do with all her things now?"

Brackenreid shrugged. "Donate them, I believe. I think she would want that."

"As long as they're preserved, I'm sure she would be pleased," I assured softly.

Holmes came back in, thanking our host for seeing us and granting us the kindness of answering our questions about such a tragic event. Brackenreid assured us that nothing about his wife's action were influenced by us, which was a nice thought but one I still doubted, to be honest.

Holmes and I strolled down the drive, planning to walk to the nearest street to find a driver.

"What did you find on your way to the washroom?" I asked.

Holmes gave me a look of mock affront. "Whatever do you mean, Watson? Why do you presume I was skulking about someone's house?"

"I presume because of a long and intimate acquaintance with you in which you regularly skulk around other people's houses."

"Ha! I may have gotten lost for a moment and found myself in Mr. Brackenreid's office," he admitted without any trace of shame.

"And in his office, believing of course that you were in the washroom, did you come across anything interesting while searching for the water and basin?"

"Hmmmm … only two train tickets to Southampton. What did you two talk about while I was turned about?"

"He is going to donate her books."

"To what?"

"He didn't say. I assume a library or museum."

We were nearing a street lined with tearooms and shops when Holmes stopped dead in his tracks, sucking in a sudden breath. "I am a complete idiot."

"Whatever do you mean?"

He drew a distracted hand across his brow, a look of self-castigation on his face. "What did you observe amongst the late Miss Stanhope's effects?"

"The normal items you'd find in any lady's purse, I suppose," I shrugged.

"You saw nothing that shouldn't be there?"

"No, I can't say that I did."

"And did you see anything missing that *should* have been there?"

I struggled to remember what Mary used to carry in her purse but could not think of any item of interest that was missing from Mrs. Brackenreid's handbag. "You'll just have to tell me, Holmes. I can't work it out on my own."

"Think. I beg of you."

"She had no fan," I offered hesitantly.

Holmes closed his eyes and drew in a slow breath. "Watching your brain work pains me at times, Watson."

"Holmes, there are many things I could rightfully point out that are painful about friendship with you, but I have the tact to keep them to myself," I snapped.

"Indeed! But since it's clear you will not reach the conclusion I am pushing you towards - she was missing a handkerchief."

"Perhaps she was not carrying one."

"I know she was." He paused dramatically. "Because I gave her mine."

Now that he had reminded me, I distinctly remembered him passing her his handkerchief that morning, the embroidered and expensive item disappearing into the curl of her palm.

"Perhaps she dropped it."

"No, she put it in her purse."

I did not remember that exactly, but I knew better than to question Holmes's recall of events. "I don't understand what this means."

He smiled, looking excited. "I can clarify that, if you don't mind a little detour before Baker Street."

We passed Baker Street, bidding the driver to let us disembark outside the bookstore from which our victim had cast herself. In the daytime, the entire street appeared much different from the dim dawn-speckled scene from the day before. The vendors were bustling, and though the area was not as crowded as the more popular London markets, there was enough foot traffic that a few people cast us curious glances as we disappeared through a narrow alley between the buildings. In the back of the building was the stair access to the roof that the desperate and confused woman had used to carry out her self-destruction.

Holmes and I made our way to the rooftop which while not precisely flat, had only a slight slope at the front of the building which still allowed one to throw themselves from the precipice. The flat ridge where the slopes of the roof met was larger than most flats, and we easily walked onto it. From our vantage in the middle of this walkable space, we could not see the street at all, but Holmes seemed uninterested in it, scouring the ground for clues. He paced back and forth, crouched low, for so long that I was sure whatever he was searching for was nowhere to be found.

I jumped a bit when he suddenly let out a sound of triumph and grabbed me by the sleeve. "Look here, Watson." He pointed excitedly to a mark on the ground.

At first, I could make neither heads nor tails of it until I hunkered down and peered closely. At once, I recognized it as a scuff made by a shoe.

"Holmes," I protested, "this could have made by anyone. Workers and chimney sweeps likely come to this roof often"-

"No," he cut me off, "this is from a woman's boot."

"How can you be sure?"

"It bears the mark of dyed suede. I deep, nearly black blue color, but distinct."

I couldn't quite make that out, but I nodded. "We know she was up here, however. So what more does this tell us?"

He gestured for me to follow him back down the roof stairway. I followed, grumbling and grunting, perhaps more irritated at my old age than anything else. Holmes ignored me admirably and, instead of turning to the opening of the alleyway, moved further behind the building, tracing the small pathways between buildings that wound towards Waymouth and High Street.

At the back of a derelict and abandoned bakery, he let out an excited "Ah ha!" and pulled the makeshift lid from a seemingly forgotten trash bin rotting beneath some eaves.

"As I suspected," he said, dipping his arm and bringing out a bundle of black material. Without asking, and despite my look of distaste, he pushed the thing into my arms. It was embroidered with lace and black pearls and I realized with a start that it was a dress, specifically the dress Mrs. Brackenreid had worn to our rooms and presumably died in.

Holmes also pulled out shoes and a handbag. An exact replica of the handbag we had examined at the morgue. Holmes snapped it open, unceremoniously dumping out the contents. Lip rouge, a mirror, a stubbed pencil, and calling cards fell out. As did a handkerchief. Specifically, Holmes's handkerchief. He reached down and snatched it up, looking both chagrined and exultant.

"Explain, Holmes," I demanded.

To my irritation, he laughed. "It's all coming together so nicely, Watson. Do you not see? Hmmm, no not yet. Well, then let's give our dear friend Lestrade a quick visit. I do believe he owes me a favor or two, and we can make this whole thing abundantly clear."

My stomach growled in protest, but Holmes, as usual, was oblivious to such fleshly needs, and I was forced once again to follow him as fetched yet another cab to take us to Scotland Yard. It was not a long drive, and as we rattled down Old Bond Street and turned left on Piccadilly, Holmes would only smile enigmatically at me when I pressed him for more details as to what we were doing. I decided to suffer in silence, hungry but intrigued by the mystery.

Scotland Yard was almost as familiar to me as Baker Street; the large, bustling structure cast in warm light and filled with well-known faces.

Lestrade's office was as messy as ever with a harangued inspector to match it. Despite this perpetual beleaguered state, the officer welcomed us in with no measure of effusiveness beyond a quick flick of his wrist and a twitch of his mouth that could have been the beginning of a smile.

"Holmes! What a pleasant surprise! I wasn't aware we had called on your services," he announced as he retook his seat.

"You did not, Lestrade." Without invitation, Holmes settled into one of the chairs across from Lestrade's messy desk. I followed suit, giving the inspector a quick, apologetic smile.

Lestrade, for his part, didn't seem put out by our presence. "So you're here for a friendly visit? Did you miss me?"

Holmes smiled brightly and, I am glad to say, sincerely. It always warmed me to see the mutual respect and, I daresay, affection that had grown between the two men. Long past were the days of Holmes making demurely insulting remarks about the inspector or finding himself on the receiving end of the older man's dismissive scorn about his investigative philosophy.

Holmes leaned back in the worn chair. "How was your holiday?"

"Lovely. Brighton is so beneficial for the constitution."

There was a strangely heavy pause, and then Holmes asked quietly, his voice carefully casual, "How is your wife?"

Lestrade's smile faltered. "Better. She's feeling much better," he told us, but I felt as if he were reassuring himself of the fact. I understood the fear of consumption, how it lorded over you like an executioner with his hand on the gallows' lever. I hoped his holiday had done her good; I hoped she recovered.

Holmes moved past the topic smoothly, his inquiry sufficient enough to allow the inspector to understand his concern. "I am in need of a favor, Lestrade." He crossed his ankle over his knee, his mouth quirking in a brief smile. He knew how much enjoyment Lestrade would derive from hearing those words from the often cocksure consulting detective.

"Hmmm. Is that right? What an odd turn of events."

"Yes, inspector, I admit it is. It is often you who are in need of a favor."

"Ha! So what is it, Holmes?"

"I need a body exhumed."

"A body? We have no unsolved murder cases open right now. Unless this is one of the instances where you stride in, take one look at a vagrant clearly drowned in the Thames, and declare that he was actually murdered by a distant relative's pet guinea pig or some such."

Instead of bristling, Holmes laughed heartily. "Still a bit sore about that giant rat of Sumatra, eh?"

"It's not likely to be forgotten any time soon."

Holmes chuckled once more. "Indeed, but I'm actually intrigued by a death that was not under any formal investigation. Mrs. Brackenreid, or better known as Miss Stanhope, evidently killed herself the morning last."

"Ah, yes. I heard you witnessed the whole thing."

Holmes frowned, evidently displeased. "In fact, we did not. We entered the scene soon after but we did not see the actual death."

"Oh, I must have been misinformed," Lestrade remarked, appearing confused. "You want to exhume this body for some particular reason or just idle curiosity?"

Holmes was quiet for a moment, then answered obliquely, "Something does not sit right with me."

"Intuition?"

"Intuition is just our mind collecting and cataloguing information at a rate too fast for us to consciously register."

Lestrade leaned back, looking discomfited. "I don't need to tell you, Holmes, that exhuming a body is an unpleasant task. And one that many families will protest against-"

"She has no family. She was an orphan," Holmes corrected.

Lestrade shook his head, his manner firmly parental. "She does. Her husband."

The detective pursed his lips, looking as if he wanted to protest. Finally, he shrugged, "He does not need to know."

The inspector cast me an incredulous look. "You expect me to approve you digging up a body without informing the family?"

Holmes sighed impatiently. "He will never have to know. Or, to be more precise, if what I suspect is true, I believe our presumptuousness will be the least of Brackenreid's concerns. Besides, you owe me, Lestrade, for that business with the Abernetty family."

A flush flared up on our host's face at the mention of that case, the details of which would surely embarrass him if made public. "Fine," he snapped, and I felt a surge of regret that we had so quickly devolved to antagonism, "I'll call in to the cemetery and morgue and have everything arranged for you by tomorrow morning." He angrily reached for a report on his desk, summarily dismissing us. Holmes stood with a brief nod, while I bid the man good day with what I hoped was an appropriate tone of contrition in my voice.

"Next-" Holmes began once we were on the kerb, but I cut him short.

"Next, I am returning to Baker Street and partaking in a robust dinner," I announced, annoyed at his strong-arming of a man I had come to view as a friend.

Holmes quirked an eyebrow at me but nodded. "Acceptable, I suppose. There is not much more we can do until morning."

At the break of dawn, we were once again heading into the morgue. And once again, Dr. Miller was waiting for us, this time with a body laid out on the wood slab that served as an examination table. Thankfully, the body had not begun to bloat, though this was soon to happen.

Miller attempted to draw us into conversation, evidently curious as to why this woman was back on his table, but Holmes brushed him off, eagerly approaching the pale body and beginning his minute examination.

I could not think of anything to say to the other doctor — small talk seemed inappropriate, and I was not in any position to provide the man with details of our inquiry since I too was at a loss as to what Holmes was searching for.

Thankfully, the detective's investigations did not take long at all.

He straightened to his full height and sighed, shaking his head. "This is not the woman who called on my services earlier this week."

I startled, taken aback by this declaration. "How can you be certain, Holmes? She was wearing a full veil."

"See here, Watson." He beckoned me closer. I stepped up the table and peered at the woman's face where Holmes was pointing. "The woman in our sitting-room purposefully stationed herself with her back to the rising sun spilling through our bow window, but even in silhouette, I could see the outline of her chin and jaw. See here." He grasped my sleeve, pulling me down until my face was nearly an inch from the deceased. He ran a finger from the line of her delicate sideburn down the curve of her jaw, barely brushing her skin. "Do you observe that light dusting of fine hair there? That was not present on our imposter." He stood, releasing me to straighten as well. "Also, she is approximately a quarter of an inch shorter." He seemed to hesitate before continuing, "She is also a bit more endowed; her dress pulled against her chest when she was laid in the ambulance. It must have been that which caught my attention that morning, though I was too slow to realize it," he admitted with a sheepish arch of his eyebrow.

I could sense Holmes's chagrin at the revelation that he had missed a vital clue due to his mind's disinclination to admit he had taken particular notice of a woman's physical attributes. I took pity on him and bypassed the discomfort smoothly, "Brackenreid wouldn't let you into the ambulance to get a closer look at the body. He merely wanted to be sure you were a witness to her apparent suicide."

He was bent over the body once more, examining her neck and arms. "The hubris," he murmured absently to himself. "There is always some action that is someone's undoing." He was shifting gently through the woman's black tresses. Holmes, while efficient and analytical during these examinations, always showed a careful respect of the dead. He turned her head with the very tips of his fingers, glancing up at Doctor Meyer. "Her hair is coming out in patches. Did you observe that, sir?"

Miller nodded. "I did. I was told she was experiencing emotional distress, so I presumed that she was in the habit of pulling out her own hair. Of course, I had little time to make any observations beyond the superficial in light of how quickly her husband wanted her buried."

Holmes shook his head. "This wasn't self-inflicted. Also, the trauma to the back of her head was not made from a fall; it is clearly the result of some sort of instrument, likely a metal rod." He slid his hand down her arms to take hold of her hand. He raised her palm to our view. "Do you also see the lesions on her side and dotting her palms? This all points to poisoning." He stood tall and stared off into space, his thoughts turned inward. He was still absently holding the woman's pale white hand in his own. I wondered what went on in that brain of his in times like these, how quickly he was rifling and shifting through information stored in that self-described attic in his mind. At last, he came out of his trance.

"I suspect thallium," he declared, as if we had not just stood for a number of prolonged moments as he did his best impression of a store-shop mannequin.

"Ingestion of thallium-" I began, but my friend held up a stalling hand.

"I did not say it was ingested," he clarified, a familiar note of impatience in his voice. "Do you remember what Mr. Brackenreid told us? That story he spun that his wife was suffering from arsenic and lead poisoning from handling her books? Well, like many lies, this was inspired by the truth." He, for lack of a better description, gently caressed the palm of the corpse. "*This* is the entryway of the poison."

The answer came upon me in a flash. "Her father's bible?"

Holmes nodded. "Why would she be handling antique books on a regular basis? Constant touching could very well ruin them. The book she likely touched more than anything in that room was her father's bible."

"But what of the head injury? You just stated she was hit over the head with a metal rod."

"Post-mortem, Watson. Clearly an attempt to create the illusion that her death was caused by a fall. A sloppy endeavor; any moderately observant person could see the difference."

Miller coughed delicately, and Holmes glanced upwards at him. "Given the time and space to thoroughly look, of course," he added judiciously. "Her death was slow; every night when she oiled that one sentimental item from her father, thallium was seeping into her skin. Prolonged contact causes skin lesions, mental deterioration, and eventually fatal damage to the nervous system and the heart."

He laid down her hand and continued, a note of ire in his voice, "He had it all planned. Once she finally succumbed, he brought her body – making sure it was in the cover of darkness – up to the roof of the bookstore and left it there before making his way to our rooms with his partner and imposter. They wanted me to be witness to both her insanity and her suicide. The woman he was with did go to the roof when he stepped into the bookstore, in front of witnesses, and then rolled the body off the slight slope. The imposter made her way back to the alley, went in the opposite direction, and quickly rid herself of the dress and shoes and bag – all made to match the victim's clothing."

"How would they have known what she'd be wearing?" I asked.

Holmes gave me a disappointed look. "Obviously, because they dressed her after she died. Just as they attempted to recreate injuries to mimic death from a fall. Of course, we know bruises can be produced even after death."

"But, Holmes," I began, remembering something, "The witnesses during the event said they saw her standing on the roof."

"Did they?"

"Yes, I asked them."

"No, did they really see this? Or did their mind fill in the details after the fact in such a vivid way as to make them believe that this is what they saw? One of your witnesses claimed Miss Stanhope held her arms aloft, but a witness I spoke to said her hands were clasped, as if in prayer."

I shook my head. "So clearly her husband arranged for her death. And he almost succeeded in getting away with it."

"He has his escape planned as well. A trip to Southampton where he could then book passage to America and be lost in the new world. I'm sure he has already arranged to have his late wife's belongings sold and the monies collected."

"Is that why he did it? For the money? Do you think he ever loved the poor woman?"

A flash of anger marred my friend's face. "I say we ask him."

Brackenreid's train to Southampton was delayed by Scotland Yard, led by Holmes and Lestrade (who had quickly forgotten his complaint against Holmes when presented with the evidence of a murder). Brackenreid had made use of a private compartment and made a sound of indignant surprise when the inspector unceremoniously slid open the door.

"Why has the train stopped?" he demanded, half-rising before Lestrade moved aside, letting Holmes step into the crowded space. His face transformed into shock, then panic, and then a strange satisfying mixture of acceptance and anger. He sat down with a thud, as if deflated.

The detective took the seat opposite at a much more leisurely pace, stretching a bit. Outside, the hustle and bustle of the platform went on as people gathered luggage, said goodbyes, and grumbled about the delay in the departure time. Lestrade and I leaned in the doorway like soldiers awaiting our orders. Holmes spared Brackenreid barely a glance before leveling those sharp, grey eyes on the female companion sitting stiffly next to him.

She, like the late Mrs. Brackenreid, was dark-haired and slight in stature, but with her face in full view, her features shared little in common with the other woman. The deceased's face, even in death, had been open, with a wide, elegant brow and deep set eyes. This woman was all angles; pretty, in her own way, particularly with her heart-shaped mouth, but she paled in comparison to the real thing. Perhaps my view was influenced, however, by the knowledge that she had helped murder her competition and had flung her body from a rooftop like so much trash.

Holmes laced his fingers together. "Your motives are not so mysterious, Mr. Brackenreid," he began as if merely discussing the weather. "Your wife had considerable wealth to her name – much more than a working barrister –

but I have a few specific questions that I'd like you to answer for me. Just two, exactly. First, was your intention always to murder your wife? From the beginning?"

I thought the man would not answer, but with Holmes and Lestrade bearing down on him, he relented. "No," he said quietly, "I sincerely thought we could have a peaceful life. She would get the children she wanted, and I would get the money to keep me comfortable."

Holmes was motionless for a long while. The train rocked lightly as passengers moved around the cabins, anxious to depart. Finally, he levelled a dark look at our prisoner. "So you were not responsible for your child's death?"

Brackenreid flinched. "Never. *She* was responsible," he spat. "For leaving him alone."

Holmes hummed so deep in his throat that it sounded like a repressed growl. "He passed in his sleep," he contended, voice filled with anger.

"And she could have saved him if she hadn't left him alone."

Holmes gave me a meaningful glance. As a doctor, I knew I could dispute his ideas; in rare cases, young babes could pass in their sleep, and there was no fault to place on anyone, but I felt something in the man's voice made arguing useless. He was set on blaming his late wife, and there was nothing anyone could say to change his mind.

Holmes seemed to recognize the same thing and asked instead, "And did you fall into the arms of another woman in your grief, or did your anger at your wife conveniently allow you to justify your infidelity?"

Brackenreid glared. "That's three questions."

"So you never really loved her?"

"I've only ever loved one woman."

Holmes hummed and turned his attention to the woman sitting silently on the bench. His eyes darted here and there over her person before he nodded to himself. He turned to Brackenreid and graced him with a humourless smile.

"Well, there's no accounting for taste, I suppose," he said simply and then rose and nodded to Lestrade to place the man under arrest.

Made in United States
Orlando, FL
24 November 2024

54351824R00093